"How do you expect to break up the lovers?"

"Does this mean you approve of their plans to marry?" Lilly countered.

"No, I do not approve," he growled. Rye's voice was intimately low, and his blatant masculinity overpowering. "But if you so much as hint that to either of them, I'll swear you're a liar. It's better for my brother to figure out for himself that your sister is nothing more than trash with money!"

The statement gave Lilly's heart a viscious squeeze. She longed to fly home that instant, but knew she couldn't until she could bring her sister with her. Her single, unengaged sister....

Susan Fox writes deeply emotional romances that will move and enthrall you—till the very last page!

Susan Fox lives with her youngest son, Patrick, in Des Moines, Iowa. A lifelong fan of Westerns and cowboys, she tends to think of romantic heroes in terms of Stetsons and boots! In what spare time she has, Susan is an unabashed couch potato and movie fan. She particularly enjoys romantic movies and also reads a variety of romance novels—with guaranteed happy endings—and plans to write many more of her own.

Susan Fox loves to hear from readers! You can write to her at: P.O. Box 35681, Des Moines, Iowa 50315, USA.

Books by Susan Fox

A Wedding in the Family
Susan Fox

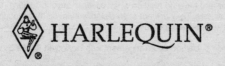

TORONTO · NEW YORK · LONDON
AMSTERDAM · PARIS · SYDNEY · HAMBURG
STOCKHOLM · ATHENS · TOKYO · MILAN · MADRID
PRAGUE · WARSAW · BUDAPEST · AUCKLAND

ISBN 0-373-03509-8

A WEDDING IN THE FAMILY

First North American Publication 1998.

This edition published by arrangement with Harlequin Books S.A.

® and TM are trademarks of the publisher. Trademarks indicated with ® are registered in the United States Patent and Trademark Office, the Canadian Trade Marks Office and in other countries.

Printed in U.S.A.

CHAPTER ONE

RYE PARRISH hated socialites.

His mother had been one of those. Rich, spoiled, obsessed with her looks, her clothes and her rancher husband's bank account. She'd hated the grand Texas house Rand Parrish had built for her. She'd endured his attentions and tolerated his companionship from time to time—as long as she could spend his money like water and live most of the year in the city.

But two sons later, she decided motherhood was too high a price to pay in exchange for the Parrish fortune. She'd abandoned her husband and sons. Walked away without a backward glance before her youngest was out of diapers and her eldest was eight years old.

Rye's younger brother, Chad, had few memories of their beautiful mother. Rye remembered everything about the glamorous woman who'd never had the capacity to show affection to her rambunctious offspring. Rena Parrish had been appalled by the dirty face and dirty clothes he'd worn after a day of play. She'd been too squeamish about his scraped knees and normal childhood illnesses to tend them. She'd never offered comfort and seldom paid either of her sons any attention. Except to criticize.

Even so, her final desertion had deeply wounded him. Her abandonment had been so absolute that he'd eventually come to hate her. But for the rest of his thirty-three years, he'd measured every female he'd ever met against her. Whatever a woman's faults or shortcomings, he'd rarely come across one whose failings were as abysmal as Rena's, rarely met another who deserved so little respect.

But the elegant blonde who walked through the small air terminal in his direction might be the rare one who came close.

Rye watched her, his eyes narrowing cynically as he noted that her collar-length blond hair had been trimmed to fall into a precise pageboy curve. Her aristocratic face was fine-boned, her features delicate, her skin a glamor-perfect peaches and cream. Her pink silk blouse and khaki bush pants were designer labels, the leather sandals on her small feet made for her by the same Italian designer who'd crafted the matching handbag. The baggage handler who carried four pieces of her monogrammed luggage followed closely, but her very erect, regal posture gave every signal that she'd dismissed his presence behind her as completely as if he'd been in charge of someone else's luggage.

Rye Parrish liked most women, but his first glimpse of this woman roused little more than contempt. Even if he hadn't guessed the little snob had come all the way from New York to Texas to express her snooty family's disapproval of her sister's engagement to his younger brother, he wouldn't have liked her. His disdain for females of her ilk ensured that.

Lillian Renard walked down the concourse, so badly disrupted by this trip to the wilds of Texas that her stomach was in knots. She'd been watching dismally out the window when the commuter aircraft began to reduce altitude, more appalled by the second at the vast emptiness of the land she'd been about to descend upon. The sparse scattering of buildings—not one more than six stories high, she'd noted—emphasized the notion that she was hundreds of miles from civilization.

Lillian didn't handle stress well. She was, in fact, a coward. Traveling to an area which she regarded as little more than a Wild West frontier was terrifying for a young woman who'd grown up in the city and had never traveled anywhere in the world that wasn't metropolitan. Why her imperious grandmother had insisted that she be the one to travel to Texas to issue the ultimatum to her rebellious younger sister, Rachel, was impossible to discern.

Except that Rachel was Grandmama's favorite. Lillian had lived most of her life scrambling to attain even a smidgen of their grandmother's approval. But Rachel, no matter how eccentric, no matter what her latest escapade or public blunder, had managed to capture the lion's share of the old woman's affection.

Until she'd run off with a cowboy from Texas. Though Rachel was barely twenty-two, Chad Parrish was her fifth love affair. But because he was a cowboy—a glorified farmer who herded cattle from horseback—their grandmother had taken exception to him. Once she'd learned he'd inherited only half of a Texas fortune, which she'd calculated to be far below her staunch requirements for her favorite granddaughter, Grandmama was apoplectic. If Rachel didn't give up her cowboy lover and return to New York, she would be promptly and irrevocably disowned.

And though the old harridan hadn't expressly decreed it, Lillian might well find herself disowned if she failed to succeed in her assignment.

Her heart trembled at the thought of being so horribly shamed. After growing up among the elites of New York, she couldn't bear to imagine the terror of being cast adrift, without a penny to her name. The scandal and humiliation of it was unthinkable. Carefully cosseted and repressibly overprotected from those her grandmother deemed unworthy, every friend she'd ever had had been ruthlessly investigated and monitored by the old lady who downright dominated everyone she came in contact with. She'd restricted the education of her granddaughters to boarding schools and colleges which catered exclusively to young ladies of impeccable breeding. A real education in something useful—in anything that might have afforded either of them a moneymaking career apart from their inheritance—had been discouraged.

Lillian was certain even that was their grandmother's way of maintaining control over her young, orphaned charges. Lillian and Rachel had been reared to supervise a houseful of servants, serve on the boards of selective charities, entertain guests on a grand scale, and make some wealthy man of Grandmama's choosing the perfectly turned-out wife. Neither of them were capable of earning a living that would enable them to maintain the rarefied lifestyle they'd been born into. The idea of either of them reduced to making their way in the world without a fortune to back them was terrifying.

Which was why Lillian had come to Texas to rescue her wayward sister. Rachel behaved as if the prospect of imperiling her inheritance was as improbable as it was untenable. Rachel had already run through huge sums of money as she'd skipped about the world indulging her whims. That she also showered her man of the moment beneath the same fountain of money she showered over herself had made her an easy target for dishonorable men with an eye to her fortune. If young Rachel were suddenly impoverished, the free-spending lifestyle she seemed to require might lead her to make desperate choices which could lead to disaster.

Particularly when Lillian considered that Rachel had landed herself in enough disasters, even *with* their grandmother's fortune to buy her out of trouble.

Lillian's aloof gaze continued to scan the small air terminal. Though she would have heartily welcomed the sight of her sister's beautiful face, she'd already resigned herself to the idea that Rachel would send someone else to carry out the boring chore of collecting her. That meant someone from the Parrish Ranch should already be on hand.

And that was surely the reason for the fresh wave of nervousness that flooded her. She was completely out of her element. She'd heard Texans were a difficult, if sometimes amiable lot. Filled with overweening pride and braggadocios exaggerations about heaven knew what in their huge, rugged state, Texans were reputed to be rough-mannered, uncouth, and nearly impossible to truly civilize, despite the size of their land, cattle and oil wealth. Grandmama had warned her implicitly about all that.

The fact that Lillian had been so closely shielded from such low-brow elements gave her an understandable fear of suddenly having to bear exposure.

And if the very tall, broad-shouldered cowboy who lounged against the next pillar was an example of the uncouth male element she'd be exposed to, she was certain she'd be terrified.

From his black Stetson to the scuffed and dusty leather of his boots, the man was a blatantly male specimen of Texas arrogance. Macho-looking in the extreme, he looked as hard and unrelenting as weathered granite. The chambray cotton of his work shirt strained over impressive chest, shoulder and arm muscles, and the soft wash-worn denim of his jeans hugged trim hips and heavily muscled thighs.

But it was the cowboy's harshly chiseled face and the almost brutal line of his mouth that drew her attention and gave her qualms about meeting his gaze. When she did, the blazing blue of his narrowed eyes made her heart skip. Even from beneath the small bit of shade his Stetson cast over his tanned face, his eyes were a hot, electric blue, their color emphasized by his dark skin-tones. That those hot, electric-blue eyes were trained on her face with the cutting intensity of a laser made her chest tighten with distress as she registered the unmistakable hostility in their hard lights.

The tightness became more pronounced, but Lillian resisted the urge to immediately look away. Some primitive sense about the man warned her not to show even a sliver of weakness. If she could brazen out his harsh gaze a moment more and get past him, she would surely find someone from the Parrish Ranch and be on her way. Suddenly, the wild, outdoor expanse of a remote Texas cattle ranch seemed far less intimidating than the man who appeared to hate the very sight of her.

She finally allowed herself to glance away, finding it surprisingly difficult to break the gleaming eye contact. Her chin went up the slightest fraction in unconscious self-defense as she continued past him.

The low, gravelly drawl that reached her before she'd got a safe distance sent a shudder of pure horror through her small frame.

"Miz Renard?"

Somehow she'd known that low, gravelly drawl would carry the unmistakable hint of insolence that it did. But how had she known it would also be so slow-sounding and rough-edged, like the warning growl of a vicious guard dog? What she hadn't known until she'd actually heard it, was that the cowboy's voice had such an appealing sensual texture beneath all that insolence and warning. The fact that it called up the image of a velvet glove covering a tight male fist didn't dampen a bit of her shockingly feminine response to it.

If this was the Texas cowboy Rachel had run off with, she could now understand a bit of her sister's rabid attraction. She also understood even more deeply how unhealthy that rabid attraction was.

Lillian brought herself to a reluctant halt, her posture going more rigid as she tried to brace herself against the cowboy's clear message of hostility. As she forced herself to turn back to him, she was terrified by the reminder that she never fared well with people who seemed not to like her. She did even worse with overbearing, domineering people. That this man appeared to possess all of those intimidating qualities badly unnerved her.

She gave a cool lift of her light brows as she tried desperately to mask the crippling insecurities she'd felt her whole life.

Her imperious, "Yes?" was meant to assert herself to him as a lady entitled to at least a pretense of outward respect. Instead, it seemed to give him license to behave in any manner he chose. That this cowboy would never lay claim to civilized manners was immediately evident.

"Figured you were Rocky's meddling big sister. Not many little aristocrats from New York blow down this way without a reason." He ignored her startled intake of breath. His insolent gaze made a head-to-toe pass over her before he reached for two of the suitcases the baggage handler carried for her.

"Here." The cases he shoved at her were neither the

smallest nor the lightest of her things. When she didn't immediately take them, he fixed her with a hard look. "No one on the Parrish Ranch is gonna carry you around on a lace pillow, Princess. Either lend a hand and wait on yourself for a change, or climb back on that plane before it flies out."

Lillian's cheeks blazed a bright red. She read the challenge in the hard shine of his eyes. His hostility was like a mile-wide wall that soared to the clouds between them. Her first instinct was to abandon her luggage and run for the safety of the airplane. Her second, that she square off with this rude, uncouth male creature and somehow best him, was even stronger.

And that ranked as the biggest surprise of Lillian's twenty-three years. As a woman who was easily intimidated, who had lived most of her life in cowardly subservience to her volatile grandmother, the notion that this man had somehow stirred some faint bit of spirit in her was stunning. That she felt compelled to fight her fears—and him—to win, was even more stunning.

He didn't wait longer than that fleeting instant of realization for her to act. He didn't give her so much as a heartbeat of time to contemplate the meaning of it all. Instead, he shoved the cases toward her a second time.

She almost lost her grip on the handle of her handbag as she grappled to take the cases without touching his long, powerful fingers. He took the other two suitcases and turned.

Just that quickly, he was striding away from her in the direction of an exit. Lillian started after him, then remembered the baggage handler. She stopped and hastily set down the cases to open her handbag for a tip. She passed the bill to the handler with a shaky smile and a soft, "Thank you," that won her an enthusiastic thanks when he saw the denomination of the bill.

By the time she'd picked up her suitcases and turned toward the exit, she saw through the glass doors that the cowboy was a distant figure halfway across the parking lot. Getting a better grip on the cases, Lillian hurried through the exit.

Once she was past the automatic doors, the heat of the blazing Texas sun struck her slight body like a speeding freight truck. The sun was so bright that she had to squint her eyes to see before they could adjust.

The wall of heat that had slammed into her now beat down oppressively. Her nervous breath began to go shallow, but she made herself step forward and walk in the direction she'd last glimpsed the cowboy.

He was no longer in sight, but she had little choice but to keep going. By the time she reached the far end of the parking lot, she was panting with frustration. She turned to scan the assortment of cars and pickups. She saw a few men with hats, but none with the battered black Stetson the cowboy had been wearing.

She ended up walking all the way back to the doors of the terminal before her arms gave out and she had to set down the heavy suitcases. Her fingers were shaking so much from the worry that she'd been abandoned in the hot sun, that she nearly dropped the cases. She did drop her handbag, scattering its contents on the hot concrete. Her eyes were blurry with perspiration as she bent to gather her things from the ground.

A wave of dizziness and nausea made her straighten and press trembling fingers to her forehead. She was an abysmal traveler, never more so than on this trying mission for her grandmother. The enormity of the task was

impacting her in the awful heat, and this shameful bout
of bad nerves was mortifying.

She didn't pay attention to the big pickup that had
rumbled to a stop along the curb a few feet away as she
struggled to relax.

"What's the matter? Are you sick?"

That low, gravelly drawl coming from so close beside
her made her jump. Resisting the urge to glance up at
the cowboy to see if the reluctant concern she'd heard
in his voice was in evidence on his rugged face, she
turned away and crouched down to gather her things
from the concrete.

"No—I—dropped my bag," she said hastily as she
picked up her wallet and cosmetics and shoved them into
her handbag. The dusty toes of the cowboy's enormous
boots intruded into the perimeter of her downcast vision.
Appalled at his nearness, she stood up.

She was about to step back to reassert the huge distance she intended to maintain between herself and this
rude man, when he caught her small chin with calloused,
blunt-nailed fingers that were too strong to fight. The
unexpected touch sent a cascade of pleasurable tingles
over her skin that made her forget her queasiness. Then,
despite the inherent power he could have used to man-
handle her, he gently forced her face up and her wide
eyes made unwilling contact with the harsh blue intensity of his.

"Your face is as white as new cotton panties."

The deliberately crude comparison he made between
her face and new lingerie insulted her. Profoundly. She
reached up and tried to push his big hand away, but it
didn't budge. She grabbed his thick wrist, but the carefully manicured ends of her fingers barely touched nail

tips with her thumb as she wrenched his hand away and took an angry step back.

"I thought the Parrish family raised cattle, Mr. Whomever-you-are," she declared with stiff dignity. "I had no idea they raised swine."

Once she'd delivered an insult to him which she considered every bit as obnoxious as the one he'd delivered her, she regained her composure. She glanced down, brushing and smoothing at her blouse and slacks, as much for something to do with her shaking hands as to recover her neat appearance.

To Rye, she gave every impression of a small exotic bird smoothing down her ruffled feathers. She already looked as neat and elegant as any other self-obsessed socialite. But to see those fine, delicate little hands fluttering around to tug and smooth over her pricey blouse and pants was almost as amusing as her priggish attempt to insult him. The sight was also powerfully arousing.

"Rye Parrish."

The sudden offer of a name identified the uncouth cowboy as the owner of the monstrous Parrish Ranch. Lillian's head snapped up and she gave an involuntary gasp.

"*You* are Rye Parrish?"

A humorless smile flitted over his hard mouth. "None other," was his terse response.

Lillian arched a brow, but said nothing. Instead, she turned from him to reach for her luggage. He got to it first, so she followed to the dusty pickup parked at the curb. She winced when he swung her cases over the side of the truck box, but he managed to set them down gently enough next to the rest of her things. The casual strength of his fit, muscled body impressed her despite her reluctance to admire anything about him. The hos-

tility he'd shown earlier reasserted itself when he opened
the passenger door of the big pickup and motioned her
in with a mocking flourish of his wide hand.

She hesitated a moment, then stepped onto the running
board and climbed into the tall vehicle. The door closed
smartly beside her the moment she sat on the seat. She
got her safety belt on by the time he rounded the pickup
and got behind the wheel.

"Ever been to Texas?" His question sounded mild
enough as he twisted the key and the truck engine roared
to life.

Lillian couldn't help that her soft, "No, I haven't,"
was wary. Particularly when his expression relaxed and
those blue eyes gave her an all-encompassing glance that
took in her neatly combed and pressed appearance. She
got the impression that her careful grooming was somehow a mark against her.

He glanced away as if he'd suddenly lost interest,
starting the pickup off to drive toward the paved road
that led to the highway. Lillian eventually made herself
relax, grateful for the truck's air-conditioning as Rye
turned onto the highway and accelerated.

She managed to feel a bit more at ease and found a
surprising amount of enjoyment in the vast expanse of
range land they passed through. Widespread herds of
cattle could be seen from time to time, but the oil pump-
ing stations that were visible from the highway seemed
to pepper the land with amazing regularity. The novelty
of speeding down the long ribbon of highway and rarely
meeting another vehicle was astonishing to someone ac-
customed to the heavy traffic snarls of New York. The
huge panorama that surrounded them was breathtaking.
The sky was as vividly blue as it was endless, and Lillian
realized with some surprise that something about the

sheer size of it all was as soothing to her as it was overwhelming.

Rye watched Ms. Lillian Renard's wide-eyed attention shift to take in every cow, oil well and change in the landscape. Twice they'd sped over the top of a shallow hill. He'd heard her soft intake of breath as they'd reached the crest. The first time, he'd thought she was alarmed by something. The second time she'd done it, he'd realized that her little gasp meant she was favorably impressed by the panoramic view of the countryside they saw briefly from their higher vantage point. He hadn't expected her to be interested in anything Texas or the Parrish Ranch had to offer.

He still didn't want to take her to Parrish. Because she was here to look down that perfectly formed aristocratic nose at his baby brother and object to his honorable intentions toward her spoiled, hotheaded sister, he didn't want her anywhere near his home.

It wasn't as if he thought her sister was good enough to marry his brother. She sure as hell wasn't. Rachel—or Rocky, as she insisted everyone call her—was very nearly the last female on the planet he could stand having around, much less wanted to see marry into his family. It had about killed him to keep his objections to himself, but he had. For his brother's sake, he'd smiled, laughed at Rocky's off-color jokes and ignored her none-too-subtle come-ons to him. He was deathly afraid that any hint of an objection from him would make his headstrong brother more determined than ever to marry her.

But now Rocky's high-toned sister was about to stick her nose into the mess. Her interference had the small possibility of spoiling everything, and Rye couldn't allow that. He didn't want anyone to put the lovers on the defensive and prompt them to an act of defiance that might end in the elopement he dreaded.

The hell of it was that his careful patience these past interminably long weeks was beginning to bear a few promising bits of fruit. As he'd hoped, Rocky and Chad were starting to appear less than enchanted with one another. Rocky, when she got worked up, had a mouth on her that could blister the hide off a hog. And she'd got worked up at Chad over a couple of little nothings the last few days. The first time, she'd pitched a fit that had sent Chad to the far end of Parrish range until the next day. The second time, his little brother had stood his ground. Rocky had taken one of the cars and gone to a honky-tonk in town, coming back in the wee hours of the morning so dangerously drunk that they'd all been amazed she hadn't wrecked the car or killed someone.

From there, Rye realized it was only a matter of time—maybe days, hopefully hours—before Chad woke up to the idea that Rocky was incapable of making him any kind of decent wife. It took every bit of self-control he'd had to allow his brother time to see it.

But now, just as he sensed Chad was on the verge of figuring it all out and calling off the engagement, here came the useless bit of fluff whose interference might coax the mismatched lovers more solidly together.

The call Rocky's grandmother had made to the ranch the day before had been their only warning of Lillian's arrival. Chad had taken the call and, believing that a visit from Lillian might soften the old lady's objections, he'd promised that she'd be met at the airport.

Chad had wanted to meet her plane, but Rye had guessed right off what the sister's sudden visit was about and insisted on doing the honors. Particularly since her grandmother had got *him* on the phone two days prior and expressed her violent objection to a marriage between their families. The female curmudgeon hadn't minced words, so there was no reason to think Lillian Renard's arrival would be anything more than a face-to-face repeat.

But the fragile-looking socialite perched beside him on the seat didn't appear capable of repeating the old witch's exact words. Now that he'd met her, he also found it difficult to believe she could come up with any demands of her hedonistic sister that would press Rocky's loud-mouthed temper toward anything more serious than laughter.

He'd felt a little like laughing himself at her stiff little swine comment. His worries over her arrival at the ranch were probably groundless. After weeks of enduring Rocky's overbearing personality and short temper, he couldn't imagine how the two females were remotely related, much less that this little pansy had the ability to bully her sister into a rash act.

Why the grandmother would send such a colorless little ninny to carry out her dirty work might have made for amusing speculation if he hadn't found her so personally annoying. Particularly when he reckoned it was up to him to derail whatever it was that she and her grandmother had cooked up. And since his only chance of doing that was to level with her and try to gain her cooperation, Rye reckoned he'd have to make a better attempt at concealing his natural aversion to her kind.

But not until he took the little snob down a notch or two. He leaned back a bit more comfortably on the seat and draped a wrist over the wheel.

"A city girl, huh?"

Rye's lazy drawl was ripe with cynical humor. Lillian glanced at his strong profile, finding his tanned handsomeness more exciting than she wanted to. The raw masculinity of the man was staggering to a young woman who'd had so little experience with men. Every instinct warned her to keep a safe distance.

"I'm certain you already know that, Mr. Parrish," she answered stiffly. The man clearly disliked her and meant to rub it in.

"And a gen-u-ine New York socialite," he drawled on.

Lillian bristled at the scorn in his tone and dared a comeback. "Is there a point to your rudeness, Mr. Parrish, or are you too boorish to realize your lack of manners? I believe it's clear enough now that the invitation for me to visit your ranch was your brother's idea. If you had such strong objections, perhaps you should have taken them up with him before my travel plans were this far along."

"What invitation are we talking about, Miz Renard?" The blue gaze that swung toward her was tinged with mockery. "I'd hardly call your grandma's *demand* to meet you at the airport and escort you to the ranch an invitation."

Lillian stared over at him, startled by his blunt statement. Her face flushed. It was just like her grandmother to do such a thing. The grim duty of delivering her message was odious enough to Lillian. To compound it by barging in on everyone uninvited was unthinkable.

Grandmama's low regard for all things rural and all things Texan had apparently disqualified the Parrish brothers from any pretense of proper manners. Rye's hostility toward her and his crudeness, though bad behavior, suddenly made sense. And because Lillian had labored all her life to be as proper and inoffensive as possible, her grandmother's actions embarrassed her.

"My apologies, Mr. Parrish." She impulsively reached out to touch his arm to emphasize her sincerity, then froze, her fingers a mere inch from his shirt sleeve. "I naturally assumed—if I'd thought you were being forced—"

She cut herself off, unable to complete the sentence. The knowledge that her grandmother would have pressured her to come anyway—and that she would have complied—kept her from offering the lie. She jerked her hand back and turned her face forward, her apprehension about coming to Texas multiplied a hundredfold.

CHAPTER TWO

RYE kept track of the highway ahead, but kept a large share of his attention on the brittle hothouse flower on the other side of the bench seat. She was truly embarrassed by her grandmother's actions. Hard, heavy blushes like the one that reddened her light complexion were impossible to fake. All the better.

"So," he went on, "Grandma sent you out here to break up the lovebirds."

The color that had only begun to ebb from her cheeks blazed back. "What makes you think that, Mr. Parrish?" she asked. She'd meant to seek a private word with Rachel to convey their grandmother's message. She'd hoped her clever younger sister could let Chad Parrish down gently and humanely. The coward in her hoped neither Parrish brother would connect her with the unpleasantness that would follow her visit. But her covert glance caught on the knowing look Rye was giving her.

"Musta been something the old gal said about crude, ego-inflated Texans." His handsome mouth quirked at Lillian's look of horror. "I thought the part about hayseed farmers on horseback was off the mark, since we're hayseed *ranchers* on horseback. But the real point your granny tried to make was that the Parrish pedigree isn't blue-blooded enough for a Renard, and the Parrish fortune is too puny for Chad to be considered a decent catch for your sister."

Lillian's soft, "Oh, no," was choked. She turned her face away as her mortification deepened. Her grandmother had clearly been as offensive to Rye Parrish as possible. Grandmama had been wildly unreasonable on the whole subject of Rachel's wedding plans, but Lillian had no idea the old lady had expressed her objections so boldly to anyone but her or Rachel.

The huge hand that suddenly gripped her thigh made her jump. The embarrassing little squeak that was surprised out of her as she whipped her head around, elevated the trauma of the day to epic proportions.

"So, judging by your granny and your equally charming sister, you Renard women don't really have any more manners or class than us uncouth Parrish men," he commented as he divided his attention between her and the road ahead. His hand didn't move.

Lillian was speechless. The feel of that big hand and its firm grip on her thigh conveyed an aggressive sensuality that took her breath away. She should have shoved his hand away, should have slapped it away. She should have slapped *him*, both for the harassment of her person and the mocking laughter in his eyes. But, frozen by the jolt of sensation that arced through her, she could do nothing but stare into his arrogant face with rounded eyes.

And that made him chuckle. It was a low, rich sound of masculine good humor. For the smallest moment, his hostility toward her eased. He dragged his hand from her thigh and slowed the pickup. She was still in an uproar from the feel of his hand, so she was only dimly aware that he was turning the truck off the highway onto a graveled ranch drive. He brought the vehicle to a halt and shifted into park before they reached the scrolled iron arch that read Parrish Ranch.

Lillian resisted the urge to shrink away when he suddenly turned toward her. The arm he laid on the back of the seat and the wrist he draped over the steering wheel made her feel claustrophobic.

"How did your grandma expect you to break up the lovers?" There was no sign of good humor now in his harsh, handsome face. The intensity in his gaze was relentless.

Lillian's everlasting cowardice warred with her flagging pride as she tried to hold up under Rye's intimidation. "Are we sharing confidences, Mr. Parrish, or are you in favor of the engagement?"

He tilted his head back slightly and his gaze narrowed on her pale face. It was obvious that he'd expected her to be easily bullied into giving a more precise answer.

"Oh, let's do share confidences, Miz Lilly," he drawled. His voice was intimately low, but his mouth was curved with a hint of menace.

Her daring, "You first," brought him inches nearer. Suddenly, she could barely stand to have him so close to her. The subtle leather and aftershave scent of him was much more pronounced, and his blatant masculinity was overpowering in the close confines. The fact that she hadn't the slightest notion how to deal with him was another distress.

She got out a hesitant, "Does this mean you approve of their plans to marry?"

The swearword he used was mild, but it was enough to startle her. "No, I do not approve," he growled. "But if you so much as hint that to either of them, I'll swear you're a liar."

The knowledge that neither of them approved of the marriage should have been a relief. It was the fervency of his threat that prevented her from relaxing.

"Why would you keep an opinion on something so important from your brother?" After living more than half her life with two relatives who made their opinions on every subject quite clear, it was a bit of a shock to think that other families practiced some restraint.

"Because it's better for my brother to figure out for himself that Rocky is nothing more than trash with money."

The brutal statement gave her heart a vicious squeeze. Her gaze fled the hard lights in his and she turned her face forward. Family loyalty should have prompted her to take offense and vigorously stand up for her sister. The bitter truth of his words broke her heart and kept her silent. She knew how wild and unprincipled her sister was. Lillian seemed to be the only member of her family who'd agonized over her sister's abominable behavior. She was probably the only one who was genuinely terrified about how Rachel would end up.

Deep in her heart, she had hoped Rachel's cowboy was strong enough to handle her, special enough to change her and inspire a more stable attitude and lifestyle. Rye's blunt assessment told her that nothing had changed with Rachel. Truthfully, Lillian would have gladly seen her inheritance and Rachel's lost if marrying Chad Parrish could save her sister from her headlong plunge toward disaster.

Rye suddenly felt faintly ashamed of himself. If he'd ever met a more fragile, repressed or proper young woman than Lillian Renard, he couldn't remember her. She was the absolute opposite of her sister in temperament and manner, and he'd taken ruthless advantage of that. He'd been predisposed to be unkind to her, but now he felt like a bully.

And that made him think of what else was in store for her. "There's something you ought to know," he said gruffly. He watched as she stiffened, and looked over at him.

"Chad didn't tell Rocky your grandma was sending you out here. He wanted it to be a...surprise."

Judging from the flash of alarm in her blue eyes before she managed to conceal it from him, Lillian knew right away what kind of reception she would get from her sister.

He looked away from her then and stared out the back glass of the truck cab. "So, if you change your mind, we can turn around and get you on another plane. I'll tell Chad to keep quiet..." He let his voice trail off.

There was nothing Lillian would have liked better than to leave Texas and fly home that instant. But Eugenia had sent her and Lillian knew she couldn't go home until or unless she could bring her sister with her. Her single, unengaged sister.

"I need to see this through, Mr. Parrish," she said quietly. "And I'd prefer to get my 'surprise' arrival over with, if that's all right with you."

"Whatever you say, Miz Lillian."

Though Rye's gruff words were suitably courteous, Lillian wasn't foolish enough to think that the rancher's attitude toward her was any less hostile. He didn't look her way once during the ten minute ride to the main house.

The next surprise Lillian had was when they finally drove over the crest of the low rise south of the ranch house. After traveling for miles through the nearly empty expanse of Texas range land, the buildings and corrals beyond the main house looked as if they stretched at least a mile wide. The sheer size of the ranch headquarters was beyond anything Lillian had imagined.

But it was the huge house that sat well to the front of it all that captured her attention. Built of stone and adobe, its red tile roof ablaze from the light of the evening sun, the house was magnificent. Six wide adobe arches stretched across the front of the one-story structure. A stone veranda beneath the roof's deep overhang divided the line of arches from the actual front of the house. Hanging pots of richly flowering plants adorned the arches and she glimpsed several groupings of black iron furniture. The wide stone veranda—and more arches—continued around both sides of the C-shaped house and suggested a size even more impressive than the front.

The obvious wealth of the Parrish home shocked her a little. Surely her grandmother had been mistaken in her judgment that Parrish money would never be enough for her sister.

"You have a beautiful home, Mr. Parrish," she offered stiffly, unable to keep the comment back. The house was truly beautiful. It would be dishonest not to tell him so.

"It's no New York mansion, but we've got indoor plumbing," he drawled, the glance he sent her way once again mocking. She searched his face for the reason.

"Is it just me you've taken an instant dislike to, or do you hate women in general?" she dared, then felt her face warm at her uncharacteristic audacity.

Rye's handsome mouth slanted. "I like women just fine, Miz Lilly," he said. "Most women, that is."

Lillian knew right away that she didn't fit into the category of most women. She'd always known that she was lacking somehow, but the rancher's clear indication that he didn't like her specifically hurt.

When he pulled the truck to a halt at the end of the

front walk, she opened the door and hastily climbed out. Recalling his "Princess" remark, she stepped onto the running board of the big pickup and leaned carefully over the dusty side of the truck box to reach for the handle of the nearest suitcase.

She hefted it out, feeling her face redden with exertion. Of course, this suitcase would have to be one of the heavier ones, but she refused to acknowledge it. Though Rye wasn't looking directly at her, she'd caught sight of the cynical twist at one corner of his handsome mouth.

Lillian as much dropped the suitcase as set it down, then turned back to reach for a second one. To her relief, the smallest case was the only one left. She glanced over at Rye in surprise, but he was already turning away to walk around the back of the pickup. He'd not only left the smallest case for her, but he'd made certain it was placed within reach.

Why that made her feel a small flutter of excitement bothered her. Rye Parrish was too big and crude and macho for her to find attractive. On the other hand, perhaps she was overreacting to his small sign of consideration. The dismal reminder that she had misread a man's intentions twice before made her wary of misreading another.

She lifted the small suitcase over the side, but when she turned to step off the running board, Rye smoothly removed the small case from her hand. He ignored her automatic, "I can carry it," before he leaned down to snag the handle of the heavy suitcase.

With astonishing ease, he strode away from her with the handles to two suitcases in each of his huge hands. He carried the heavy load as if he were carrying nothing more challenging than four handbags, and Lillian was impressed in spite of her natural aversion to muscular men.

She followed him up the front walk and stepped beneath the deep roof overhang that shaded the veranda. She hurried past Rye to open the door, then held it for him as he carried her cases into the house.

The icy chill of the air-conditioned house was a welcome relief from the outdoor heat. Rye walked on, leaving her to close the door and take a quick look around as her eyes adjusted to the dimmer light.

The large sunken living room that began a few feet from the tiled entry was part of the center portion of the huge home. Along the wall opposite the entry were two wide doorways. The door on the left led to what looked to be a large, well-appointed kitchen with commercial-size appliances. The delicious smell of food cooking made her mouth water. The double doors on the right opened to a formal dining room to reveal a long, polished table. Lillian could see the deep shine from where she stood.

The living room itself was decorated with heavy leather and wood furniture that complemented the rough timber beams that striped the ceiling. Brightly colored Native American rugs decorated the dark lustrous wood of the floor, drawing out the vivid colors of the Western paintings on the white walls.

It was a room that could have come directly from the pages of a glossy decorating magazine and she was duly impressed. Though it was worlds removed from the formal elegance of her grandmother's homes, which she'd always felt had a sterile look, the colors and arrangement of this room were as visually interesting as they were inviting. In spite of her reluctance to come here, she couldn't wait to see the rest of the huge home.

The only thing that spoiled the view was the rancher who'd paused at the wide hallway to the left to glance back at her. "You comin'?"

With nothing more gracious than that, he disappeared through the doorway, the heels of his boots thudding confidently on the rug runner in the hall.

Lillian followed him down the west hall of the ranch house. Halfway to the end, Rye turned and stepped through an open door with his load. Seconds later, Lillian walked into one of the loveliest bedrooms she'd ever seen.

The room was larger than she expected. Decorated with three large leafy plants that were nearly as tall as she, the room was utterly feminine. Gauzy ivory fabric was draped in deep swags from the high points of the four-poster bed and above the French doors to the inner patio. Heavy, intricate lace lay elegantly across the dark polished wood of the dresser, chests and night tables. The area rug was a soft peach shade on the wood floor, but the walls were decorated with cheery watercolors of flowered scenes. Two antique oval pictures were hung tastefully, the attractive women in the sepia-toned photographs clearly Parrish matriarchs. Though the old photos made it impossible to detect eye color, the dark hair and facial structure of each bore a faint resemblance to the present day owner of the Parrish ranch.

Lillian looked quietly at the old pictures, intrigued by what she could only describe as the feminine ruggedness of the two frontier women. Rye's low voice drew her attention.

"Bathroom's over there." He gestured to her right. He walked over and put out a hand to draw back one side of the gauzy drapes over the French doors. "Patio and pool out that way. This room is the other half of the

master suite.'' He released the drape and nodded toward
the door to her left. ''Other half's through there and
mine.''

She'd glanced obligingly toward the closed door before the ''and mine'' fully registered. When it did, her
gaze swung back to meet the gleam in his.

''If you get spooked by something howlin' in the
night, or some low-to-the-ground critter wanders in, I'll
be handy.'' The faint curve of his mouth gave away his
exaggeration.

Lillian felt a stir of annoyance at his none-too-subtle
effort to put her off. She arched a brow. ''Unless you're
claiming responsibility for your nocturnal habits ahead
of time, Mr. Parrish, I'm certain I'll be fine.'' The stiff
smile she managed mirrored his as she maintained contact with the remarkable blue of his eyes.

It was oddly satisfying to see the brief spark of surprise on his face before his expression hardened. The
hostility she'd sensed in him earlier reasserted itself as
he strode toward the hall door.

''Dovey's waitin' supper. We'll eat when you get
done primping.'' With that, he walked into the hall and
pulled the heavy door closed behind him.

Lillian, a veteran of her grandmother's impatience,
checked her appearance in the bathroom mirror, ran a
brush through her hair, then washed her hands and
rushed out to the hall. Once there, she slowed and
walked quietly toward the living room. The stillness of
the home, despite its size, gave her the sense that Rachel
was nowhere close by.

Though her nervousness about intruding on her sister
wasn't particularly high at the moment, she couldn't help
the undercurrent of dread she felt. The thought that she'd

be spared the fallout from the "surprise" of her arrival for a little longer put her more at ease, though a part of her wanted to get it over with as soon as possible.

She was tired of walking on eggshells around her family. She was weary to death of being the hapless target of someone else's bad temper. The fact that she'd sensed a vast potential for bad temper in her reluctant host sent her spirits downward.

On the other hand, the reminder that she was obligated to tolerate only so much from nonfamily was welcome. There was an end to her forced contact with Rye Parrish. In as little as a few days, she'd be on her way back to the airport and civilization. The idea made her feel better.

She entered the large living room and walked toward the sound of voices coming from the kitchen. She'd almost reached the door when what she heard made her hesitate.

"You ain't said much about what she's like, boss," a gravelly male voice was saying.

A child's voice cut in, "Is she bratty and mean like Rocky?"

The question pained Lillian, but the silence that followed made her strain to hear what Rye would say.

"Don't you need to take that bowl of food out to your pup, Joey?" There was a mild rebuke in Rye's tone and she could instantly imagine the stern look that went with it.

Joey's voice was suddenly subdued. "Yes, sir. I'll do it now."

Lillian heard the hiss of a sliding-glass door as it opened and the thud when it closed. She'd just taken a step toward the kitchen door when Rye spoke again.

"She seems as pampered and useless as any other

female of her type,'' he said grimly, ''but she's more a sissy than a brat. She'll probably fall over in a faint if her hair gets mussed or her clothes get wrinkled.''

Lillian felt heat surge into her cheeks as the other man chuckled. Rye went on.

''I'd just as soon we kept Joey away from her. And keep Buster away from her, too. Hell, she's probably never been around a dog you couldn't put a bow on or hold in your hand. God knows how she'd take it if he got too close or he jumped up on her.''

''Ol' Chad sure picked up a burr,'' the gravelly voice commented.

Rye said nothing more. Lillian was outraged, but the shame she felt was just as strong. It distressed her to think Rye Parrish had so accurately pegged her. She was nothing if not a sissy. What other kind of woman would have allowed her grandmother and sister to walk all over her for so many years? She hadn't exactly been pampered, though by his standards she probably was. She was fairly useless as far as supporting herself or making her own way in the world, but her careful grooming and attention to her figure had been an absolute necessity. She didn't dare appear less than perfect. He was even right about big dogs.

He was not right, however, about keeping the child away from her. Though she'd rarely had an opportunity to be around children, she felt no animosity toward them. It hurt that he thought he needed to protect a child from her.

On the other hand, the boy's comment about Rachel being mean and bratty probably meant he was worried that she'd behave the same way. The notion that Rye might be sensitive to the boy's feelings and that he was perhaps trying to protect the child made her a little less angry.

Lillian forced her mouth into a pleasant line, then stepped forward, letting her sandals make a quiet tap-tap on the wood floor to alert everyone in the kitchen that she was about to walk in.

The kitchen was even larger than she'd expected. The cook was in the midst of meal preparations, but he'd confined the various utensils, pans and serving dishes he was using to his immediate work area. Though the room was predominantly white, it had a surprising amount of color, from the assortment of pans that hung over a center island counter to the collection of cookbooks, knick-knacks and potted herbs arranged here and there. The view of the patio and pool beyond the sliding-glass doors added even more color to the generously proportioned room.

The dining area of the kitchen was spacious enough for a large round oak table and chairs, as well as a small sofa and recliner. The room boasted a wall-mounted TV next to the wide door to the dining room and was placed high enough that it could be seen from anywhere in the kitchen.

Rye sat at the table, his plate, napkin and silverware pushed toward the middle of the table so his coffee cup could sit closer to the edge. He nodded to her when she walked in, then spoke to the cook.

"Here she is now, Dovey."

The cook was a short, muscular, middle-aged man with a well-tended crew cut that gave the impression he'd been in the military at one time. Lillian gave him a smile as Rye stood to his feet and introduced her.

"Miz Lillian Renard, meet Dovey Smithers. He

mostly cooks, but he also runs the house. Dovey, this is Miz Rocky's older sister.''

She made her smile widen as she crossed to the cook and offered her hand to shake his. Dovey hastily wiped his hand on a nearby dish towel so he could shake her hand.

"I'm right pleased to meet you, Miz Renard. Hope you enjoy yer stay with us.'' He released her hand then added, ''Now if there's any kinda food you'd like to have while yer here, or if you'd rather have somethin' other than what I've cooked, don't you be afraid to say so. Ain't no one goes hungry when I'm doing the cookin'.''

Rye spoke up. "If she's as particular as Miz Rocky, you might have to turn into a short-order cook to keep them happy, Dovey.''

Dovey gave his boss a mock frown, but his dark eyes twinkled good-naturedly. "Now, boss, this little gal looks about as sweet and easy to get along with as vanilla icing on a white cake.''

Lillian was prompted to speak up. "I'm certain whatever you've planned to cook will be fine, Mr. Smithers. In fact, what you've prepared now smells wonderful.''

"Name's Dovey to you, Miz Lillian. If you'd like to sit down, I'll get supper on the table—unless you'd rather I set the table in the dining room. Won't be no trouble if you'd rather eat formal.''

Lillian shook her head, but her soft, "In here will be fine,'' was nearly drowned out by Rye's brisk, ''The hell it's not.''

The silence that followed was awkward and loud. Lillian felt her face go hot. "I wouldn't be comfortable making more work for you...Dovey.'' She gave him a nervous smile. "I'd prefer not being formal if there's a choice."

Dovey sent Rye another frown. "See there, boss? She's as easy to get along with as she looks." The cook hurried around the island counter to the table and pulled out the chair next to Rye. "If you'd like to sit down, Miz Lillian..."

Lillian walked to the table and slid obligingly onto the chair he held for her, murmuring a soft, "Thank you," once she was seated.

She offered a stiff smile to Rye, who watched her almost warily, then she glanced toward the news report on the television. The sound was on low, but she could easily hear it.

The swish of the sliding door drew her attention and she turned her head in time to see the boy try to squeeze through the opening without letting the pup in. But the pup, a short-haired black and tan breed with huge feet, who was more the size of a small pony, was determined to wiggle in.

"Buster!" the boy shouted as the animal shoved past his legs and burst into the room.

Buster—who was more a muscular dog than puppy—barked loudly at Lillian then suddenly lunged toward her, his dark eyes wild and his huge mouth hanging open to show lethally sharp teeth.

As alarmed as she was appalled, Lillian sprang from her chair to use it as a barricade. The huge puppy pounded around the chair, yapping hysterically as he tried to catch her. She'd let go of the chair to dash around the table, when a thickly muscled arm slid around her waist and lifted her off her feet to swing her out of harm's way.

"No."

Rye's command wasn't exactly a shout, but it rumbled in the large room. Though Lillian was held high against his side, she was watching when the monstrous puppy skidded to a stop on the vinyl floor, his paws slamming up against the toes of Rye's big boots.

"Down."

The puppy reacted to the second command as if he'd been shot. He instantly dropped down at Rye's feet and gave a soft whimper before he looked up at the stern rancher with no less than adoration in his big brown eyes.

"Good dog."

As if he knew he was forgiven, the dog opened his huge mouth and let his tongue roll out in a goofy parody of a smile, but he didn't offer to get up.

Meanwhile, Lillian's heart was pounding, as much from the amazing feeling of being held so effortlessly against Rye's hard-muscled body as out of terror about the dog. He'd picked her up as if she weighed nothing and the sheer manliness of the protective gesture made her insides quiver.

"Gosh, I'm sorry, Rye. I didn't mean to let Buster get in." The boy's face was the picture of anxiety.

Rye swung Lillian past the huge dog and set her on her feet next to her chair. His gruff, "Under the table," made the monstrous young dog crawl swiftly beneath it and settle against one of the claw-foot legs of the wood pedestal.

Lillian, still a bit shaken, brushed self-consciously at her clothes, smoothing out the tiny wrinkles of her blouse before she ran her hands down the upper thigh of her slacks. She'd just raised her hands to run her fingers over her hair when the heavy silence in the big kitchen registered.

Her heart dipped a bit as she slid a quick glance toward Rye. Heat scorched her face as she noted the intense way he was looking at her. She knew then that he'd been watching every move she'd made. When his gaze met hers, the gleam of amusement that shone in their blue depths was a shameful reminder of what she'd overheard him say earlier about mussed hair and wrinkled clothes.

When he suddenly glanced from her to the boy, he gave the impression he'd somehow dismissed her.

Lillian's wide gaze shot from Rye's harsh expression to the boy's pale face. The child was obviously terrified, and her heart went out to him. She suddenly decided Rye Parrish might be a bully. His next words were a complete surprise.

"I don't want Buster to eat our houseguests, Joey. Let's see to it he sticks to dog food."

The effect Rye's words had on the worried little boy was astonishing. Lillian was watching when the child's tense face relaxed and he broke into a huge grin. A quick glance toward Rye showed that his grin was just as big.

The sound of the boy's giggles brought an instant smile to Lillian and a lightness of heart that surprised her. That was the moment she forgave Rye for his rudeness to her. If he was always as patient with the boy and his dog as he'd been these past minutes, then he wasn't quite the uncouth boor he tried to be.

Unfortunately, that made him more appealing to Lillian than was prudent.

CHAPTER THREE

"Miz Lillian, this is my cousin, Joey Parrish," Rye said, then motioned the boy to step closer. Joey complied, but stopped at arm's length from her while Rye finished the introductions.

"Joey, this is Miz Lillian. She's Miz Rocky's older sister."

Joey's mumbled, "Pleased to meet ya, ma'am," charmed Lillian.

"And I'm pleased to meet you, Joey," she said with a gentle smile as she held out her hand to shake his. "That's some dog you have there. Is he a good playmate?"

Because her first instinct was to make the boy feel comfortable and to let him know she was friendly, she'd tried to add as much pleasant interest as she could to her response.

Joey shyly took her hand and gave it one firm shake before he let go and pulled back.

"He's my friend," he said with childish candor as he wedged his fingers into the front pocket of his jeans. His straight golden brown hair came to his collar in a sleek cut and framed a small, freckled face that was surprisingly angelic. His large, thickly fringed hazel eyes sparkled with an engaging mixture of earnestness and intelligence as he looked up at her, and Lillian liked him instantly.

Before she could think of something else to say that would make them both feel more at ease, Rye said gruffly, "Go ahead and sit down, Joey. Dovey's waitin' to serve."

As if relieved to get away, Joey turned from her and rushed around the table to the place set for him. Lillian sat down and reached for her napkin as Rye sat and moved his coffee cup out of the way to drag his plate and silverware closer.

Dovey served a layered lettuce salad, fat baked potatoes, fresh tomatoes and thick sirloin steaks that had been broiled medium-well. Generous slabs of steamy homemade bread that had been buttered and broiled on one side rested on the slim edge of their large dinner plates.

Lillian couldn't help but be privately appalled at the huge plate of food. After more than half a lifetime of having her food scrutinized by a grandmother who disdained anything but small portions, she felt uncomfortable with such large servings.

"Something wrong with the food?"

Rye's brusque words startled her. Lillian automatically glanced his way, saw the disapproval that tightened his jaw, then quickly shook her head.

"No—not at all," she said, then made herself smile and look over at the cook, who was wiping down the counter. The way Dovey's gaze shot away from hers— as if he'd been listening, but didn't want to be caught—made her realize he might be worried about whether she liked his cooking.

She hastily added, "It all looks so wonderful, I can't decide where to start." She was rewarded with a broad grin and a wink from the cook.

She looked down at her plate, straightened the napkin on her lap, then reached determinedly for her knife and fork.

*   *   *

Lillian managed to follow Rye's and Joey's lead and clear her plate. Actually, the food had been so good that she'd been a bit shocked at how easily she'd packed it away. But later, as she sat on a lawn chair on the patio, she felt elephantine. She could almost hear her grandmother chiding her for making a pig of herself.

Actually, her grandmother would have done more than merely chide her. "Lillian, I will not tolerate a fat child." How many times did she still hear her grandmother's blunt reminders about gaining so much as an ounce of weight?

In truth, Eugenia Renard had an extensive list of things she would not tolerate. It still hurt to know that the list seemed to be comprised exclusively of the things she might have wanted to do or try. But the harshest items on the list had to do with Lillian's looks.

The sudden plunge of her spirits made Lillian force her thoughts away from that subject. She turned her head to glance toward the shallow end of the pool where the boy was, and gasped.

The huge pup—Buster—had been sitting silently beside her. He'd been so quiet, she'd not known he was there. To turn her head and come face-to-face with the brute startled her badly. Coupled with his loud, "Woof," she sprang up from the lawn chair.

Rye stood in the ranch kitchen watching out the patio door. He'd been looking on as the dog slipped up beside Lillian and sat down beside her. He'd been waiting with secret amusement to see what she'd do when she discovered how close Buster was. He had no worry about the dog, who clearly seemed smitten by the new human in his territory. The old nursery rhyme about Little Miss Muffet made a singsong pass through his mind.

Suddenly, "Miss Muffet" turned her head, saw the dog, then shot up off the lawn chair as if it were spring-loaded.

Rye chuckled, then got tickled again as he watched Lillian eye the big dog while she kept the lawn chair between them. He told himself it was because of Joey that he decided to rescue her. The boy was sensitive about the dog, and if Miz High Society raised hell, it would upset them all.

Just as he was about to slide the big door open and step out, he saw Lillian stretch a small hand toward Buster. Though he could see the tremor in those delicate fingers, the fact that she was making even a small over-ture toward the dog surprised him.

Buster's big mouth dropped open and his tongue rolled out to give those timid fingers an enthusiastic lick, but Lillian snatched her hand back. The distaste on her face as she looked down her perfectly formed little nose nettled Rye.

He slid the door open, stepped through, then let it slide quietly closed. His low whistle got Buster's atten-tion. The big dog turned from Lillian, and bounded to-ward him. He allowed the animal to dance excitedly around him a moment before he leaned down to give him an affectionate rub around the ears and neck.

Rye's gruff, "Where's the stick?" and the brisk wave of his hand sent Buster charging to the far end of the patio and through the open gate. Rye straightened, his gaze going immediately to Lillian's. The look of near fascination he'd caught before her gaze fled his gave him an odd little tingle.

More than once he'd caught those haunting blue eyes looking at him, watching him. Though he didn't consider himself a vain man, he knew female attraction when he saw it. The little aristocrat must have found something about him worth watching, but he didn't feel flattered. Women like her had nothing more exciting to offer a man than tantrums and hellish salon and boutique bills. Sex was simply a means to manipulate or coerce, and love for anyone beyond herself would be impossible. He'd be damned if he fell into the same trap his father had.

"My brother called a few minutes ago," he said, then hesitated when he realized how harshly he'd spoken. It was surprisingly hard for him to soften his tone. His "Rocky decided she wanted to hare off to Dallas," was only marginally better. "Better entertainment there, I reckon."

Lillian ignored his sarcasm, but nodded stiffly. "Has he told her I've arrived?"

"No tellin' what he's told her."

Because he sounded so irritable, Lillian felt about as welcome as the plague. She glanced away a moment and resisted the urge to fidget. Lord she hated to have intruded on this man. Not because he was a gracious host, because he certainly was not, but because he seemed to have a singular talent for making her feel unwanted.

Considering the fact that she'd felt that way most of her life, it didn't really surprise her that this uncouth stranger behaved no differently toward her than did the members of her own family.

It seemed she would never be free of that mysterious something that kept others from feeling affection for her—from even liking her. Though sometimes she was convinced it was possible to die from lack of love, the fact that she'd survived this far without much of it made her believe she could go on a good many more years the way she always had.

Overwhelmed by emotion suddenly, she glanced determinedly toward the boy, who appeared to be struggling with one of the little sails on his boat. She forced out a hoarse, "I think the boy could use some help," then started off toward the far end of the pool.

But by the time she reached the boy, he'd straightened the sail and had stepped down into the shallow end of the pool to set the boat on the water. He was so absorbed in what he was doing that Lillian stopped a few feet away so she wouldn't disturb him.

The colorful little boat dipped awkwardly when Joey set it on the water. He started it off with a push that sent it gliding across the surface before water resistance slowed it to a stop. By the time it did, he was wading after it.

Left without an excuse to linger nearby, Lillian turned and strode back to the lawn chair. Rye had apparently not taken his eyes from her the whole time and his calm scrutiny was unnerving. She was too edgy now to sit down.

"The boy seems quite competent at what he's doing. I should have realized," she said, feeling the kind of screaming awkwardness that made her wish she could be more at ease around others.

Unable to bear the penetrating look Rye was giving her, Lillian glanced away a moment, then reluctantly brought her gaze back to meet his. "I'm certain my presence here might be...is...inconvenient. Surely there's some sort of hotel or motel in the area." She hesitated when his dark brows drew together in clear displeasure. "When Rachel returns from Dallas, we could just as easily have our visit there."

He was shaking his head before she finished, and one corner of his handsome mouth curled. "I figured you'd at least wait until you actually got hot and dusty and bored, before you started whining to leave.''

Lillian felt the insult like a slap. The urge to slap back was shockingly strong. "I imagine nearly every place I could go in Texas is hot, dusty and boring, Mr. Parrish, but I never whine. However, I do know when I'm not welcome. If the situation were reversed, you'd do the same.''

Something dark flared in his eyes and the mocking curl of his mouth tightened. "If the situation were reversed, you'd damn well put up with me until I'd got done what I came to do.''

"And that's the difference between us, I suppose," she said quietly. "The fact that you're ungracious enough to inflict your cranky disposition on others until you get your way is hardly a surprise. But I don't behave that way, and I never appreciate putting up with that trait in others.''

The fact that Rye actually chuckled at her made the color in her face darken. "You might not behave that way, but my guess is you've had vast experience putting up with people who do, whether you 'appreciate' it or not.''

Lillian didn't reply to that. There was no reason to. The man had obviously figured it all out. How could he not? He'd met her sister, and her grandmother had made an especially witchy impression on him over the phone. All in all, there was probably no hope that any of them could ever get along with one another, much less that the friction between her and Rye could ease.

"Nevertheless, Mr. Parrish, I think it would be better for me to take a room someplace else. I'm certain we'll both be more comfortable.''

"Something tells me your granny wouldn't give a

rat's backside for the comfort of anyone but herself. How will you explain moving to a motel forty miles down the highway when she expects you to be here?''

Lillian felt her face go hot again. ''Thank you for your concern, but I'm afraid that's my problem.''

Rye's fine mouth moved into a smirking line. ''Honey, if you can't put up with me, you sure as hell won't be able to put up with your little sister when she shows up. She might have been bad before, but in the few weeks she's been around here, she's gone downhill.''

A sick feeling went through her. ''What do you mean by...downhill?''

Rye was watching Lillian closely, had been all along. He saw clearly the flash of anxiety that made her beautiful blue eyes go silver for the tiniest moment. Was her anxiety for her sister or for herself?

He didn't let himself be kind. ''Unless you can tell me that your sister is normally spiteful and cruel, that she hates kids and animals, and is prone to drink, swear and come on to every male over sixteen who crosses her path, then I'd say she's gone downhill.''

He heard Lillian's shaky intake of breath and saw the sudden pallor that bleached the color from her cheeks. He'd shocked her. She glanced toward Joey, who was playing with his boat. Rye was watching when he saw the nearly imperceptible straightening of her narrow shoulders. Her shock was still there, but under rigid control by the time she turned her head and looked directly at him.

''Your description of my sister makes me wonder what kind of man your brother must be to want to marry her.''

Rye didn't let her see that her barb had hit home.

"Many a man falls for a beautiful face and a sexy body and thinks he's found the love of his life. Eventually, he realizes he's fallen for a pretty shell. And, that the pretty shell hides a world of ugliness."

Lillian couldn't seem to get a full breath. Her fears for her wayward sister were stronger than ever. It was one thing to acknowledge to herself that her sister had distressing faults. It was quite another to hear someone else bluntly chronicle them.

"I would like to go to that motel," she told him. "Tonight, if it can be arranged."

Rye nodded. "I need to use the phone first for a business call. Then I'll get you the number and you can see if they have any rooms left." His mouth tightened grimly. "Tourists, you know."

Lillian said nothing, but stepped around him and walked with stiff dignity toward the patio door.

Rye rarely bothered to manipulate others. He never needed to. Not when he could get what he wanted by buying it, giving an order or using persuasion. Lillian Renard was too rich to be bought off or bribed. She was no employee, so he couldn't order her about, and yet, she wasn't the kind of woman he cared to finesse or persuade. But now that everyone knew she'd arrived on Parrish, he couldn't allow her to leave. It would raise too many questions.

Which was why he'd called the three nearest motels, charged their dozen or so available rooms to a credit card, then later gave their phone numbers to Lillian. She'd seemed so embarrassed when she'd had to tell him that there were no motel vacancies that he'd almost felt ashamed of his little trick. Almost.

Now she was in her room for the night. He'd heard

the shower going, but she'd turned it off a few minutes ago. The strip of light he saw beneath the door that connected their rooms told him she was still up.

He'd got Joey to bed, but Buster had been too restless to stay in the boy's room. Rye had let the big pup out to run, certain he'd come back sometime before morning, scratching at a door to be let back in.

It wasn't until he saw the strip of light beneath the connecting door go out that he turned off his own light and went to sleep.

Lillian rarely slept well in a strange bed, but it wasn't just the unfamiliar bed that disrupted her sleep this time. Her mind was spinning with a thousand thoughts, few of them calming. Worry for her sister, anxiety about her grandmother's volatile mood, and the memory of her stern host's animosity toward her and her sister made Lillian toss fretfully on the bed in the darkened room, unable to rest.

The soft whir of central air-conditioning masked most of the night sounds—insects chirping, a dog's howl— but ironically it wasn't the night sounds that made her edgy. It was the lack of sound. No traffic, no stereo or TV playing someplace...

Lillian eventually drifted off. She was dreaming about the huge pup, dreaming he was chasing her. The dream was so real that Lillian awoke with a gasp and bolted upright in bed.

The patio lighting illuminated the gauzy drapes that hung at the French doors and lit the bedroom dimly. The bed jiggled, and the low woof that came next unnerved her and made her peer warily toward the foot of the bed.

The huge black shape that suddenly leaped on the bed was terrifying. Lillian's startled cry lodged in her throat.

She could see well enough to tell it was the boy's dog, Buster, but at just the moment she was about to calm herself and reach for the switch on the bedside lamp, she caught sight of another dark shape on the bed. She heard a distinctive rattle...

Rye heard the piercing scream. He'd never heard anything so hair-raising in all his life. The high-pitched sound brought him instantly awake, and he was out of bed and halfway to the connecting door before he knew what he was doing.

In the next second, the door flew open and a small satin-clad figure bolted through the opening. Pausing only long enough to slam the door shut, Lillian dashed blindly into him, hitting him with enough force to knock him off balance.

His arms came up reflexively to catch hold of her waist, but she'd already recovered enough to grab him around the neck. Her small body literally shook and she made desperate little sounds that reminded him of Joey's night terrors. Before he could get a firm grip on her, she planted her bare foot against his shin and, heedless of propriety, she levered herself high against him. Her cheek bumped his and left a smudge of wetness as she hugged herself tightly around his neck. The amazing combination of tear splatters and sharp little fingernails on his bare back made his spine tingle.

He had no choice but to put his arms around her. "What the hell is wrong with you?" he growled. Her first response was to wrap herself even tighter around him and shake more violently. He tried to pry her away, but a series of terrified sniffles made him stop.

A scratching sound on the connecting door made her whimper and try to look over her shoulder toward the door. Buster whined plaintively from the other side and Rye suddenly realized what had spooked her. He couldn't conceal his disgust.

"Hell, it's just the pup," he groused, then renewed his effort to peel her off the front of him. His big hands fastened on her sides. His thumbs brushed the undersides of her satin-covered breasts, but he ruthlessly ignored them. He tried to gain an inch between them, but her arms were locked tightly around his neck.

He turned his head to speak directly into her ear. "In case you didn't notice, lady, I sleep in the raw and your nightie is about as thick as tissue paper." To emphasize his meaning, his hands slid down to her hips. His fingers splayed over the rounded softness of her bottom and flexed meaningfully, bringing her so firmly against him that the thin satin nightgown concealed nothing.

It aggravated him when nothing changed. It was as if she hadn't heard a word, because she clung to him just as tightly as before. That was when he noticed how soft she felt against him, how feminine. She smelled sweet and exotic and her fine golden hair felt like silken threads against his cheek and shoulder.

His arousal came on so suddenly and powerfully that he actually swayed. He *hurt*. He tried again to push her away, but the flash fire of emotion that roared up when she held on made him turn toward the bed.

Lillian was hysterical. She was shaking so badly her body ached. She was tongue-tied with fear. She couldn't make sense of Rye's irritable growls, she only knew that the hard feel of him, his masculine scent, and the low rumbling sound of his voice made her feel safe.

She sensed somehow that he was fearless. And perhaps because she'd so often in her life been afraid, she was desperate to cling to someone who was not. Oh, God, the craving to wrap herself in Rye's solid strength and somehow become as fearless—as confident in being safe—as he was drove her those several moments.

She felt him move, felt him turn and walk away from the door and the horror on the other side. The next thing she knew, she was lying on her back in Rye's big bed, pressed into the mattress by the weight of his body. He hesitated only a moment before his warm lips found hers.

The rough, masculine kiss was forceful and carnal, jolting her out of her hysteria. Rye pressured her lips open and swept inside, penetrating and devouring her mouth so voraciously that Lillian gasped for air. She felt the snap of her gown's spaghetti strap as his big hand slid beneath the bodice to settle over her bare breast and toy aggressively with its tip.

The incredible sensations that arced through her body sent a tingling sweetness from her nerve endings to the deepest, most feminine part of her. Lillian felt herself melt and was helpless to keep from returning his kiss. Her compliance seemed to enflame him. She felt him surge against her and his kiss became more aggressive. She was drowning, losing herself in the most astonishing sensations she'd ever experienced. The most astonishing, and the most frightening.

Lillian pulled her arms from around his neck and tried to brace her hands against his chest to lever him away. His hands moved down her sides, then slid beneath her to grip her backside as he moved erotically against her.

Lillian cried out, torn between fresh horror at his aggression and the swift piercing arousal that sent sizzling bolts of pleasure through her. She could feel his hot skin against her in places that were far too intimate and knew they had to stop. Before she was completely over-whelmed, Lillian managed to push at him. She was so close to being swept away by the wonderful and terrible things he made her feel, so close, so close...

Rye pulled back only far enough to growl down into her face, "What's the matter, Princess? Change your mind?"

Panting from arousal and a need for air, Lillian stared up helplessly into the shadowed face over hers. Now that he'd broken off the kiss, her mouth ached for the pressure and dominance of his. His hands were moving slowly from the places they had been and Lillian had the shocking urge to grab them and force them back to what they'd been doing. Her body was vibrating with real pain. It took a moment before she realized that the fine tremors that went through his big body were a signal of frustration and rage.

Rye shoved himself off her. He swore viciously and Lillian shrank into the mattress, mortified when she realized that the hem of her gown had worked itself hip high. Bent on escape, she rolled away. Struggling to pull down her nightgown, she scrambled off the bed. She fumbled for her broken strap in the darkness, then gave up and clutched the front of her gown.

"There are several names for a tease like you." Rye's voice was grim. "Every single one I can think of is foul—"

"T-there's a s-ss—" Lillian tried again to speak, tried to drown out the cruel words he was saying, tried to redeem the horrible situation that had somehow become more horrid, but her teeth were chattering and she kept biting her tongue.

She jumped when he growled, "There's a dog in your

room, is all. A damned puppy, big as a horse, but harmless, and not worth a minute of lost sleep.''

She got out a shaky, ''N-no. A sn-ss-ss—'' She heard the bed give a soft groan when he vaulted off the mattress and started swearing again. Her next try, ''There's a sn-snake,'' was drowned out by the sound of a drawer jerked open, then slammed shut, and more swearing.

Lillian felt her shaking abruptly stop as realization struck. Rye Parrish not only didn't like her, he loathed her. It was as if the sudden knowledge made her insides shrink. A man who'd known her less than twelve hours *loathed* her. The shaking started again.

Fearful of staying in his room another second, but just as fearful of returning to the horror in her own, Lillian moved shakily toward the hall door. She searched for the doorknob, found it, then quickly let herself out into the darkened hall.

She sought refuge in a guest room off the hallway. Still terrified and perhaps still irrational, she hastily inspected the room.

She knew the rattling sound she'd heard earlier had been made by a rattlesnake. Even she had seen enough ''Bonanza'' episodes to know what a rattlesnake sounded like. The sound, coupled with the snakelike shape on the coverlet of her bed had sent her screaming to Rye for rescue and protection.

Fresh tears stung her eyes. Instead of safety and help, he'd thrown her down on his bed and kissed her like a sex-crazed barbarian. And, oh, God, she'd kissed him back. Kissed him, felt things she'd never imagined she could feel, but before she'd been swept totally into insanity, she'd tried to stop him. She'd been right to stop him, to stop herself.

The memory of the loathing in his voice when he'd

called her a tease wounded her. The fact that he'd refused to listen to what she'd been trying to tell him was a stark demonstration of how much contempt he felt for her as a human being. The knowledge that she was somehow living a nightmare made her feel faint.

When she was certain the bedroom was safe, she retreated to the room's bed, carefully checked it, then pulled back the coverlet and top sheet to climb in. She placed a pillow between her back and the bed's headboard, then pulled the coverlet to her chin and tried to stop shaking. If she could survive until morning, she'd find some way to get into her room, get her things, then flee this hellish place.

If she'd had even an inkling of how traumatizing this trip would be, she'd have found some way to avoid it. For the first time in her life Lillian realized there were worse things than her grandmother's wrath.

The moment Lillian fled his room into the hall, Rye opened the connecting door and let Buster into his room. He closed the door, but didn't bother to turn on the light. He simply wadded the jeans he'd got from a drawer and threw them toward a chair. He gruffly ordered the dog to lie down by the patio doors, then climbed into his bed, his body still roaring with frustrated desire.

Rye laid in the dark a long time, staring into the black shadows. He couldn't get the little princess out of his thoughts. Damned if he couldn't still smell her, couldn't still taste her on his mouth. And that choice little body. He'd never in his life had such a violent, fiery arousal, never dreamed sex urges could be that powerful, that compelling.

Hell, he'd almost had sex with her. The memory of how close he'd been, how good it had felt, then how physically devastating it had been when she'd suddenly rejected him, made him break out in another sweat.

Because his senses were still razor sharp, a new scent began to make an impression on him. The dusky musk was familiar and he felt a coldness gust over him as he recognized what the scent was: rattlesnake.

Rye turned on his side and braced himself on an elbow to reach for the lamp switch on the night table. He glanced quickly at the carpet next to the bed, then got up and crossed to the chair for his jeans. Buster was on his feet in an instant and the musky smell suddenly got stronger.

Rye was staring down at the dog when the sick feeling of intuition struck. He yanked on his jeans, then turned toward the connecting door.

Had Lillian gone back into that bedroom? He'd been so worked up, he hadn't listened too closely. Buster smelled of rattlesnake. The monster pup had scared her by somehow getting into her room, but that didn't mean a snake had gotten in, too. It probably just meant that Buster had had a go-round with a rattler—one which he'd won, or he'd be lying dead somewhere, snakebit.

His nerves on edge for an entirely different reason, Rye grabbed a flashlight from a drawer, then hurried toward the connecting door.

Lillian hadn't returned to her room. Once he got the light on and got a look at her bed, he knew precisely why she hadn't.

There on the coverlet was one of the biggest rattlesnakes he'd ever seen, its head missing, its long thick body dusty and mangled from being dragged around.

Buster bounded past him, jumped into the center of the bed and sat proudly next to his prize—the prize he'd presented to Ms. Lillian Renard as a token of canine affection.

CHAPTER FOUR

LILLIAN sat on the bed in the silent guest room with every light on, and pulled the coverlet higher. She couldn't seem to quit shaking. She heard someone walk down the hallway and cringed when she recognized Rye's confident stride. She listened tensely as she heard him knock on first one door, then another as he worked his way down the hall.

His low-voiced, "Lillian?" at each one as he continued moving in her direction made her ragged nerves jump. She called out a shaky, "In here," that brought him straight to her door.

When she heard him stop, she called out, "You have snakes in your house, Mr. Parrish."

As if she'd insulted him, Rye opened the door a crack, hesitated, then shoved the door wide. He stood in the opening wearing nothing but an old pair of Levi's.

Lillian was suddenly flooded with the memory of how it had felt to cling to that tall, hard body, of how unexpectedly wonderful it had felt lying beneath his naked weight in the middle of his bed. She could still feel the heat of his bare flesh against hers, could still taste his kiss. The memory of his lips crushing and dominating hers sent a shock of excitement through her. Lillian's eyes were riveted to him.

As if he'd read her mind, Rye's expression darkened. "Buster brought you a kill. An honor of sorts to show affection. The snake's dead."

Lillian kept silent, doing her best to conceal how repelled she was by what he'd told her. He went on.

"I disposed of the snake, shut Buster in the garage for the night, and Dovey is stripping the bedclothes off the bed you were using. Though I don't expect you'll have the nerve to sleep in there again, he's putting on fresh bedding in case you change your mind."

The slant of his lips suggested how remote he considered the possibility. Lillian sensed the challenge that ghosted through his rough tone and felt her face pale.

Oh, God, could she go back into that room and actually *sleep* in that bed? As she stared over into Rye's harshly chiseled face, she could almost read the word "sissy" in the blue gleam of his eyes.

Hoping to solve this unexpected dilemma, she ventured a quiet, "But I've already used this bed."

Rye's lips twisted a bit more. "For about a half hour, is all. Spread it up and it'll be good as new."

He couldn't have made his expectations clearer and Lillian's heart sank. She looked down a minute at the coverlet she was clutching beneath her chin, then forced her gaze up to meet his full-on.

"I-I'll think about it," she got out, then endured the skeptical nod he gave her. He glanced briefly down the length of her body beneath the coverlet before his blue eyes came up and burned into hers.

Suddenly, she wanted to go back to New York, back to the familiar life and surroundings that had no arrogant Texas males with macho attitudes, hard muscular bodies or lethal levels of testosterone.

To New York, where handsome, civilized men looked through her and rarely approached. New York, where men of breeding and refinement would never dream of throwing her down and kissing her with the male knowledge and expertise Rye Parrish had. To New York, where she'd not only be safe from him, but would perhaps be able to forget the storm of sexual excitement that sent tiny bolts of pleasure through her—just because he was looking at her that way.

"Unless you'd feel safer in *my* room."

His low sexy words took her breath away and turned her insides to mush. Lillian couldn't take her eyes off him. It was as if he'd read her mind and knew how appalled she was by him—yet how wildly hungry for his attention she was.

Unable to force the words of a refusal past the surprising dryness in her mouth, Lillian gave her head a shake.

His gruff, "Good night then," sent a wave of longing through her that made her shiver.

He reached for the doorknob, then hesitated. "I owe you an apology for calling you a tease. My mistake." As if that made everything all right, he backed out of the room.

She watched him go, unable to ignore the magnificent play of his bare shoulder, arm and chest muscles before the door closed with a quiet click.

Lillian trembled beneath the covers, her heart pounding. So this was what lust was like. This intense, irrational, violent craving for something your body was suddenly convinced it could die without.

It was a long time before Lillian calmed down enough to fall asleep.

She slept until ten the next morning and awoke to the sound of the boy's voice down the hall from her door.

She found a robe on the back of the bathroom door in the guest room, then stepped into the hall and hurried back to her original room. She'd meant to get some things and return to the other guest room to get ready for the day. But once she saw the lovely bedroom and saw for herself that no traces of the last night's trauma remained, she decided to use it instead.

She emerged a bit later, her hair neatly combed, the right touch of makeup applied and the tailored blue slacks and blouse she had on looking fresh and crisply pressed.

Now that she'd been awake long enough to remember the entire incident the night before, she was mortified by her hysterical actions. The memory of how she'd flung herself at her host and climbed all over him, made her insides twist with horror. Only the knowledge that she'd have to face him sometime—and somehow reestablish herself as a reserved, well-behaved young woman of breeding—made her continue down the hall to the main part of the house. The sooner she got the difficult next meeting with Rye behind her, the more comfortable she'd be. At least until her sister returned to the ranch.

Dovey greeted her the moment she stepped into the kitchen.

"Mornin', Miz Lillian. Sorry about the trouble in the night," he said, his friendly face creasing with sincerity.

Lillian smiled. "Thank you so much for restoring the room to order, Dovey. One would never know."

Dovey's eyes got rounder. "That ol' rattler was about as big as we ever see around here, that's for sure. Fool pup likely pushed open that French door from the patio. Musta not been latched just right."

Lillian nodded and gave a brave smile.

"Would you like your breakfast now?" he asked her next.

"It's late enough, I can wait for lunch," she told him,

then glanced out the patio door to the pool area. Buster was standing in the shade of the roof's deep overhang, a stout chain fastened around his big neck as he peered eagerly through the patio door, his entire attention focused on Lillian.

She looked toward the cook. "I wouldn't mind coffee, if it's already made."

"Comin' up," he said as he got out a cup and quickly filled it. Lillian stepped over to the counter to take the cup. Dovey nodded toward the patio as she tasted her coffee. "Ol' Buster's in a lot of trouble, which is why he's tied up today. The boy was pretty upset when the boss told him about it at breakfast."

Lillian glanced toward the pup, suddenly worried.

"Nothing will happen to the dog, will it?"

"Can't say for sure, o' course," Dovey said. "I do know that this ranch is wide enough for a big rowdy dog like that one, long as he's not a danger to people or livestock. So it depends on if the boss thinks draggin' dead rattlers into the house is a danger." The cook shook his head. "Joey's aunt already made it plain that she doesn't want Buster if she takes in the boy again come fall, so ol' Buster's about at the end of the line. If he can't get along out here, he won't have no place else to go."

Curious, Lillian asked, "Then Joey doesn't normally live with his parents?"

"Joey's mom and dad were killed in a wreck just after the first of the year," Dovey told her. "Joey and Buster were living with his mom's sister, but he and the pup together were a little rambunctious for the aunt's two little girls, so the boss invited Joey to spend the summer on the ranch." Dovey gave a fond chuckle. "This place is a paradise for boys and dogs. Open spaces, lots to do, all kinds of places to explore...'' He let his voice trail off as he wiped down a counter.

Lillian looked through the patio door at the huge pup, who had started to bark. The moment he saw he had her attention, the animal began to yip excitedly and jump at the end of his chain. She couldn't imagine allowing a dog of his size and energy to live indoors or to be confined to a yard or an outside pen.

She was reminded of her own dog, and the memory made her sad. Lillian had been only a little younger than Joey when her parents had died. The tiny Yorkshire terrier their father had given her at Christmas a couple years before had been small and well behaved, but that hadn't kept Grandmama from giving the animal away. ''I don't know what possessed your father to allow that abominable creature into the house,'' she'd declared.

Lillian had been heartbroken by her grandmother's refusal to let her keep her pet. And though she'd begged to know whom the dog had been given to, her grandmother had refused to tell.

Over the years, Lillian had come to suspect that instead of giving her little dog away to a good home, her grandmother had had the animal destroyed. In spite of Buster's rowdiness, Lillian suddenly felt anxious to intervene on the pup's behalf, to save Buster for little Joey as she'd been unable to save her own pet.

Perhaps she could speak to Rye and somehow make certain he would keep the dog. Surely there were dog obedience schools in Texas where Buster could be trained to be an asset to the ranch. Dogs were used to herd sheep, but could they also be used to herd cattle? If the boy had to be separated from his pet, surely the separation would be less wrenching if he knew his dog was alive and living on the Parrish ranch.

Feeling strongly enough about it to brave seeking Rye out, she set her coffee aside and asked, "Is Mr. Parrish nearby this morning?"

The cook looked up from the counter. "I b'lieve he's down at the stable. I can get someone to show you where he's at." He paused to add proudly, "The boss owns some of the finest horses in this part of Texas, if you're interested."

Lillian couldn't conceal her pleasure. "I'd love to see them, but I doubt we need to bother anyone to escort me. If you could send me off in the right direction, I'm certain I can find Mr. Parrish on my own."

In no time, Lillian was on her way. Dovey had insisted on fitting her with a wide-brimmed Stetson before sending her out in the hot sun, and she was grateful for it almost right away. Though it was not quite eleven in the morning, the sun was blazing.

Once she was away from the shelter of the big house and patio, she could hear the sounds of the cattle and horses scattered about the headquarters. The nearer she got to the corrals, the more dust swirled in the hot air. She soon spied the stable and walked toward it. She was still a distance away when a commotion from inside another barn drew her attention.

A magnificent chestnut stallion bolted out the door of the other barn, his lead rope swinging free. Two cowboys gave chase, but the horse smoothly eluded them. As if the stallion were teasing his pursuers, he stopped and stood statue-like long enough for one of the men to touch the rope. The moment he did, the stallion lunged sideways, yanking the rope safely out of reach.

In the next instant, the horse whirled and bolted down the lane in Lillian's direction. Lillian stared those first seconds, taking in the splendid sight of the beautiful

horse as he raced toward her. Though the lane wasn't
too narrow, the board fence along each side of it served
to channel the runaway straight toward her.

While the stallion was still several feet away, Lillian
reached up and took off her hat. She moved to the center
of the lane, stretched her arms away from her sides and
waved the hat to block the horse's path.

The animal continued toward her, but just when she
was about to jump out of the way to avoid being run
down, the big horse slid to a dusty halt in front of her.
Peeved at being stopped, the stallion reared. Lillian did
her best to appear unintimidated by the horse's choler.
After a tense moment, the stallion dropped down on all
fours. Lillian simply reached forward and caught the
lead rope. The horse didn't fight her, though he pranced
fretfully and tossed his head a time or two.

"What a beauty you are," she said delightedly, then
laughed a bit when the huge animal gave her a nudge
with his big nose. "And don't you know it," she murmured as she rubbed his cheek.

The two cowboys approached cautiously, but Lillian
called out, "Would you mind if I took him back to the
barn?"

Rye's deep voice rumbled from behind her. "I mind,
but it doesn't look like either you or the horse gives a
damn that I do."

Lillian glanced over her shoulder at the rancher, who
was walking swiftly toward her. He was virtually glow-
ering. He nodded toward the horse. "Do you really
know your way around horses, or was getting your hands
on that lead rope just dumb luck?"

She ignored the insult and forced a cool smile. "We
have a few horses back where I come from, Mr. Parrish.
Equestrian skills are considered an asset." She turned

back to the stallion, who was still fidgeting a bit, and stroked his nose. Without waiting for Rye to say more, she coaxed the horse into a turn and led him confidently toward the barn.

Rye followed, then directed her to the huge stall at the far end of the barn. Once she'd put the horse inside and latched the stall gate, the stallion put his head over the top rail and nudged her hand in a demand for more attention.

Rye stopped a scant few inches away, and Lillian was screamingly aware of his nearness. Memories of the night before overwhelmed her, undermining her fragile confidence in ways she didn't completely understand. She felt a new kind of vulnerability in Rye's presence, and knew instinctively that her vulnerability was sexual. Being alone with him suddenly seemed the most dangerous thing she could do, and her heart begin to race.

"H-he's a beauty," she told Rye, and stroked the stallion's sleek neck.

"He's a handful," Rye remarked.

"Do you use him for ranch work or just for stud?"

"Depends on the time of year."

Clearly, he wasn't going to offer much in the way of conversation. She'd hoped to be able to approach the problem of the pup with a bit more finesse. Lillian glanced his way briefly, and felt her face heat when she saw the intense way he was staring at her. Her nervousness suddenly multiplied, and it took her a moment to recall why she'd sought him out.

When she did, she gave the horse a last pat, then stepped back from the stall, as much to put distance between her and Rye as between her and the horse. "I was wondering about Buster and what will happen to him."

Rye's expression hardened. "Why? I suppose you expect me to put him down."

Her lips parted in horrified surprise. "N-no—no—of course not. The animal isn't a serious threat to anyone. After all, the snake was dead." She hesitated when he glanced away from her as if what she'd said had irritated him. She watched his stern profile and took note of the agitated flex of his jaw. She dared a quiet, "A child's pet should be given every opportunity."

That brought his burning gaze back to hers. "Why should you give a damn about either the boy or the dog? Unless you think I'm a heartless s.o.b."

It startled Lillian that he'd guessed her secret worry—that he really was some sort of heartless…jerk. She had been afraid that he might act too harshly toward the dog, which was why she'd sought him out.

"I'm sorry," she said quietly. "You obviously have a problem with my concern." She turned away to start for the door in hopes of making a quick escape to the house. His gruff voice stopped her.

"I thought females like you only cared about themselves."

Lillian glanced back at him. Rye stood looking at her, his arms crossed over his wide chest in a way that made him look every bit the arrogant, domineering male he was.

His assessment not only hurt her feelings, it made her angry. She gave him a stiff little smile. "Go on believing whatever you like. I doubt you're a man who changes his mind easily anyway."

She was about to walk away a second time, when he spoke. "Don't you want to know what I'm going to do about the dog?"

Lillian turned toward him a bit more and tried to prepare herself. She suddenly sensed there was something hard and cruel and unforgiving in Rye Parrish, something that warned her not to trust in any gentleness or compassion that might also be a part of the harsh man he was.

She was almost too cowardly suddenly to get the words out. "What will you do?"

"Just what I've done. Shut him in the garage overnight, and chain him up for the morning. He'll be off the chain as soon as I go to the house for lunch. That meet with your approval, Princess?"

Lillian stared at the tough expression he was giving her, completely confused by him. "And the boy gets to keep his dog?"

"As long as he stays on Parrish, Joey can keep his dog. If he has to live with his aunt Jenny in the fall, Buster will have to stay here."

Relieved, Lillian had just started to smile when he growled, "And that's more than someone like you has any business knowing."

The small smile died on her lips. For a moment, she'd caught a fleeting glimpse of something soft behind the stone facade her host seemed determined to present to her. His last remark was clearly her punishment. Her soft, "Thanks for telling me anyway," wasn't much louder than a whisper. She turned away from him then, and walked quickly to the house.

Lillian, Rye and Joey had a quiet lunch in the kitchen. The tension between the two adults seemed to keep the boy subdued, though Lillian did try to draw him into conversation a time or two. They'd almost finished eating when they heard the sound of the huge front door opening.

Joey excused himself from the table and raced to the kitchen door to see who it was. Once he did, he abruptly turned to hurry toward the patio door. He stopped with his hand on the latch and glanced Rye's way. "Can I go now, Rye?" At an almost imperceptible nod from Rye, the boy yanked the door open enough to squeeze through the opening before he was outside and the door hissed shut.

With some surprise, Lillian noticed Dovey take off his apron, then quietly exit the room via the door to the dining room.

The loud, "Anybody home?" that boomed through the house made Rye send her a look and say, "Ready or not, Princess." He eased his chair back but didn't get up as he called out to the visitor, "Come see for yourself."

The sultry sound of Rachel's, "Hey there, cowboy," as she reached the kitchen door made Lillian freeze inside. The fact that her sister was in a good mood—good enough to flirt with her fiancé's brother—was a sure sign that she still hadn't been told about Lillian's visit.

Lillian rubbed her lips with her napkin, so filled with dread suddenly that she wanted to disappear. She happened to glance Rye's way, saw that he was watching her, then tried to relax. Surely her sister wouldn't have a full-scale tantrum in front of her fiancé or Rye. Sarcasm might be more Rachel's style, though a few acid comments from her younger sister might actually be worse than a tantrum.

In the end, Lillian braced herself for the worst, knowing full well Rachel always behaved exactly as she pleased. She glanced toward the door and pasted a neutral smile on her lips as her sister swept through the doorway.

Rachel Renard was a beauty, with red hair, porcelain skin and jewel-blue eyes. Her weeks in Texas seemed to have enhanced her beauty. She was a woman who prided herself on her remarkable looks and took great care to not only dress in a manner that called attention to herself, but she behaved in ways that guaranteed she wouldn't be overlooked.

Rachel was halfway across the floor in a beeline for Rye before she caught sight of Lillian. "Lillian!" Rachel stopped in the middle of the floor. The surprise on her beautiful face changed so suddenly to outrage that it was as if someone flipped a switch. "What are you doing here?"

Lillian managed to retain her smile. "I'm here to meet your fiancé."

"Liar."

The venom in Rachel's voice stunned her, but before Lillian could do more than give a small shake of her head, Rachel seemed to calm down. She smiled coldly and said, "Lillian says she's here to meet you, Chad."

Lillian knew what was coming. Nevertheless, she got to her feet and glanced Chad's way. Chad Parrish was tall and handsome, a younger, much milder version of Rye.

Her soft, "Hello, Chad, I'm pleased to meet you," was all any of them were able to say before Rachel went on.

"Yes, Chad, I'm certain she's pleased to meet you. Lillian meets so few men on her own." Rachel chuckled at the blush that crept into her sister's cheeks. "But then, Grandmama isn't finished making Lillian presentable. She's had braces to straighten her teeth, surgery to straighten her nose and Eugenia's 'gentle' guidance to make certain she knows how to behave like the bloodless little mannequin she wants her to be.''

Lillian's gaze flew from Chad's to her sister's. "Rachel, that's eno—''

"The problem is," Rachel went on, her voice going a defiant shade louder, "Lillian will never be exactly as Grandmama wants her to be. But that's because our father had an affair the year he married my mother. An affair that produced Lillian.''

Lillian's choked intake of breath barely gave her sister pause.

"So instead of me being an only child, I've always had this odd, older half-sister.'' Rachel stopped then and smiled at Lillian's confusion.

Lillian couldn't make sense of what Rachel had said, but it was clear that the younger woman was furious and meant to slice her to bits in front of the two men. As usual, she never knew how to stand up to Rachel in a way that was effective. She tried a calm, "I think the two of us should speak in private.''

Her quiet words set her sister off again. "I think it would be much better for the two of us to speak in public, you little hypocrite. You came to Texas because Eugenia sent you here. She's using you to scare me into line with talk of disowning me, isn't she? You're here because you think that if you succeed, Grandmama will be grateful and she'll finally feel some affection for you. But,'' she added with certainty, "that won't ever happen.''

The silence that fell was charged. Chad spoke up then. "Hell, Rocky, that's enough.'' He reached over to touch Rachel's arm, but she threw off his hand and hissed, "No, it's not enough.''

Lillian was tongue-tied with mortification and disbelief. The difference in her sister—how much worse she had become—was so stark that it took her breath away.

"Someone should have told you the truth a long time ago and put you in your place," she went on. "But then, if you'd known, Eugenia might never have had such a pathetically devoted granddaughter. No one was supposed to tell that you were Daddy's bastard daughter or that he expected my mother to pass you off as her own and raise you if she wanted to stay married to him."

Lillian was so shocked by what her sister was saying that it was a moment before she could get out a bewildered, "What?"

"You little prig," Rachel said scornfully as she advanced toward her, "always so stiff and proper. As if your pretty manners really make you better than everyone else."

Lillian stood unmoving, barely breathing as she tried to take it all in. The shame of having such scandalous revelations stated baldly in front of strangers made her feel ill, but the revelations themselves dominated her attention. She and Rachel didn't have the same mother? How could Rachel know something that important and Lillian not?

And yet Lillian knew instantly that her sister was telling the truth. The mysteries that had secretly plagued her for a lifetime stirred in her stunned mind. Their mother had always favored Rachel, showering her with attention and affection, while mostly ignoring Lillian and behaving coldly toward her. That unhappy fact of life might have destroyed Lillian as a child if their father hadn't been so loving toward her and if he hadn't hired a nanny for each of his daughters.

Rachel had been Mommy's girl, but Lillian had been Daddy's. Lillian had been eight years old before she realized how wrong that was. Her parents had died in the air crash by then. But now to suddenly find out her mother had not really been her mother...

"God, somebody catch her before she faints." Rachel's mocking words hit her like a hand across the face. She realized dimly that Chad had rushed to her side and slipped his hand beneath her elbow and that Rye had got to his feet.

Chad's soft, "Miss Lillian?" penetrated the fog of shock. Lillian turned her head and looked into Chad's handsome face. The gentle concern in his dark eyes was almost her undoing. She wasn't used to such concern, such compassion. It amazed her that a complete stranger could feel them for her.

"I—I'm fine."

Rye's voice was low and rough. "Chad, maybe Miz Lillian would like to rest in her room."

Lillian shook her head. "No. No, thank you," she said, then looked over at her sister. "I'd like to speak to Rachel. Privately."

Rachel's lovely face flushed. "I've said everything to you that I want. Go on, be the perfect little errand girl and call Eugenia. Tell her that she and her cronies will be getting their wedding invitations in another week or so."

With that, Rachel turned and stalked from the kitchen.

CHAPTER FIVE

THE kitchen—the whole house—seemed to shudder in the aftermath of Rachel's fury as she stormed through the living room to the hall. The sound of a guest room door opening, then slamming shut was the proper end for the scene she'd inflicted on them all.

The silence in the kitchen was prolonged and excruciating. Lillian was too mortified to look directly at either brother. She brought her chin up a fraction and said quietly, "Apparently my sister felt there were some skeletons rattling around in the Renard closet that suddenly needed air. My apologies."

Chad's gentle, "Miz Lillian?" made her look at him. "Would you like a cup of sweet coffee?" he asked. "Kinda settles the nerves."

Now Rye spoke up. "Miz Lilly could probably use something stronger."

"No, thank you," she said quietly, then dared a quick look in Rye's direction. Her gaze shot away from the intent way he was staring at her.

"Would you like to sit down?" Chad asked her next, his hand still on her arm as if he had to steady her. She edged slightly away from him to break the contact.

"No, I'm fine." Lillian felt the terrible awkwardness that always placed her at a disadvantage with others.

Chad shook his head and gently reclaimed her arm. "You still look pale, Miz Lillian. Maybe you ought to rest a bit, while I have a talk with Rocky. I'm sorry for her—her little tantrum. I don't know what gets into her sometimes. She didn't have cause to light into you thataway.''

He was so nice to her, such a gentleman, that Lillian suddenly felt guilty. She'd come here to separate her sister from this man because Eugenia didn't think he was good enough for her favorite granddaughter. Though Lillian had been in Chad's presence only a brief span of minutes, she knew the reverse was true—her sister would never be good enough for Chad Parrish.

''Thank you for your concern, Mr. Parrish—''

''Chad,'' he insisted and smiled.

Lillian nodded and tried a small smile of her own. ''Thank you, Chad. I'll be fine.''

''Are you sure?''

Rye cut in. ''I'll keep an eye on her.''

Lillian glanced at Rye, but Chad drew her attention back to him when he said, ''I hope we can get over this rough patch, Miz Lillian. I'd really like you to have a good visit with us.''

She couldn't help that she was completely charmed by Chad Parrish. The smile she gave him was much less forced. ''Thank you. I'd like that, too.''

He nodded. ''See you later on,'' he said, then turned and walked from the kitchen in the direction Rachel had gone in.

Once he was out of the room, Rye spoke.

''I admit, I never thought of that angle.''

Lillian looked over at the stern set of his handsome face. ''Pardon me?''

He gave her an unamused smile. ''I didn't think about the possibility of you seducing him away from Rocky.''

Lillian stared at him a moment, then felt her face heat as his meaning sunk in. ''As I'm certain you can see, I hardly have what it takes to seduce any man away from my sister."

"You fish for compliments just like any other princess," he remarked cynically. "My brother is usually partial to blondes. He's also a sucker for a woman in distress. You should have let go of a few tears and thrown yourself into his arms."

Lillian blushed painfully at the reminder of the night before. "I don't manipulate people with tears, Mr. Parrish. Would you mind if I use your telephone?"

"So you do need to report in?"

"If I don't, Eugenia will call here soon. I'll use my phone card to avoid running up a charge to your phone."

Rye's expression hardened. "You'll dial the number and save the phone card for another time."

"I carry a phone card for times like this."

"You're a guest."

Lillian gave him a skeptical look. "I'm an intruder, Mr. Parrish. I'll use the phone card."

"Suit yourself. There's a phone in the den. East hall, first door on your left."

Rye turned from her, got his hat off a peg, then let himself out the sliding door to the patio. Lillian watched him stride across the patio toward the gate.

The east hall of the ranch house was just as long as the west hall where Rye's room, hers, Joey's and four other bedrooms were. The den was the first door on the left, but there were four others, one of which she assumed might lead to Dovey's quarters.

Grandmama Eugenia was surprisingly tolerant of Lillian's report.

"I guarantee Rachel will give this whole matter more careful consideration than she's given anything in her life," Eugenia declared, then added with blunt pride, "She might be spirited and headstrong, but she's bright."

Sensing her grandmother was finished with the conversation, Lillian spoke up.

"Rachel mentioned something I need to discuss with you, Grandmama," she said as firmly as she dared.

"And what is that?" the elderly woman demanded, reverting to her usual brusqueness.

Because she knew she would be cut off if she didn't get right to the point, Lillian rushed out with, "Rachel said that our father had an affair, and that I'm not Margaret's natural daughter. She said Daddy demanded that Margaret raise me as her own."

The phone line was so silent that Lillian was certain they'd been disconnected. She forced out a soft, "Is it true?"

Eugenia, whose temper often surpassed Rachel's, asserted in a cold, crisp tone, "Rachel needs to learn some harsh lessons. Tell her I expect her to be on hand for my call tomorrow. I will be unhappy if I'm unable to reach her then. Be certain you tell her that."

The fact that Eugenia had ignored her question was a small shock. "But what about—"

"I will speak to you then, as well."

The line went dead. Lillian slowly lowered the receiver and placed it in the phone cradle. The knot of dread that had been growing inside her tightened painfully.

Eugenia was furious with her. It wasn't the kind of fury that boiled up suddenly and was quickly vented, but the more frightening kind that fumed in silence, building until it was at its most destructive before it was set loose. Lillian had witnessed that kind of fury in her grandmother only a handful of times, and it terrified her to think Eugenia might be that upset with her.

When Lillian emerged from the den, it was almost two in the afternoon. No one seemed to be around, though she could hear the low volume of the television in the kitchen. She hesitated in the living room, uncertain about whether or not to seek her sister out when she heard the rapid tap of Rachel's boot heels coming down the hall from the opposite wing of the house.

The moment Rachel strode into the living room she glared at Lillian, then turned and continued on to the front door. The handbag she was carrying was slung over her shoulder and she had a lit cigarette in her hand.

Because Rachel still looked furious, Lillian knew it was futile to speak to her. She could only watch as Rachel threw open the front door and stalked out. This time, she didn't slam the door shut after herself, but left it to swing wide. Lillian walked over to close it.

When she reached the door, she saw Rachel climb into a sleek little car. Rachel slammed the car door, started the engine, then sat revving it mercilessly. She glanced toward the house, saw Lillian still standing at the door, and smirked.

The engine roared again, but this time, the car took off, its tires digging gravel from the drive and throwing it in a spray as the car shot away from the end of the sidewalk. Lillian was about to close the door when she heard the car horn blare, the sound of a hard thud, then the tortured yelp of an animal.

Alarmed, she rushed out the door in time to see Buster twisting on the ground in the wake of the flying gravel and dust as Rachel's car roared on down the drive. The injured dog was trying frantically to get to his feet, his dark coat matted with dirt as he struggled.

The horror of it made Lillian cry out. She turned to shout for Dovey, then ran to where the poor animal writhed on the ground.

The pup's eyes were glazed with pain and he was panting in agony by the time she reached him. She was on her knees beside him in an instant, and tried to hold him still. She glanced back toward the house and yelled again for Dovey.

It was then that she saw Joey. The boy had just come running around the corner of the house when he saw her bending over his dog. Lillian turned her body to shield the sight of the injured animal from the child.

"Joey, find Rye," she called to him, desperate to keep him away from the dog. When he started to run toward her instead, she shouted a desperate, "No! Please find Rye—hurry!"

But Joey's whole attention was focused on his dog. It was as if he hadn't heard a word she said. Fortunately, Dovey came jogging toward them and he intercepted the boy before he could get to the dog.

From there, everything happened at a nightmarish pace. Rye appeared out of nowhere. He pulled Lillian out of the way and got to his knees to check the dog. Lillian heard the sound of an engine and turned her head in time to see one of the ranch hands pull up in an old station wagon.

With the ranch hand's help and the use of a blanket, which they used as a stretcher, Rye got Buster into the back of the station wagon. Joey wiggled from Dovey's hold and launched himself into the back of the vehicle to sit beside his dog. A moment later, Rye climbed out of the back.

"I need someone to drive or someone to help with the dog," he said as he looked at Dovey.

Lillian glanced at the terrified little boy and spoke up. "I'll help with the dog." She was about to climb into the back of the car when Rye caught her arm. "That's no place for a princess."

"And it's no place for a little boy, either," she retorted, then yanked her arm free and climbed in alongside the dog.

Rye slammed the tailgate shut and ran to the driver's side of the car to jump in. They were roaring off to the highway in seconds. Relieved the dog was still alive and that they were on their way to help, Lillian did her best to reassure the boy while she did what she could to make the dog comfortable.

"Please, Buster, don't die!" Joey was saying as he buried his face in the fur of Buster's dusty black neck.

Lillian was surprised to find her eyes were stinging as she held the dog steady and laid a consoling hand on the boy's small shoulder.

"But I want to go with him," Joey insisted as Lillian tried to prevent him from following Rye down the hall to the vet's operating room. Because Rye and the vet had all they could do to carry the injured dog without hurting him more, he'd given Lillian charge of the boy.

"Please—I gotta know if he'll be okay," Joey insisted. Joey was trying so hard to keep his brave face and not cry, but the tears were there behind the haunted look in his eyes.

Unable to deny the boy, Lillian got a firmer grip on his hand and started down the hall with him. Surely they could watch from the door for a few moments, long enough to hear something from the vet.

They reached the room Buster had been carried into, then stood in the doorway. Lillian got down on one knee and kept Joey close to her side. The vet's assistant came into the room from another door. Rye and the vet laid the big pup on the table, but it took all three men to keep him quiet for a quick examination.

Buster yelped and Joey reached for Lillian, his arms going around her neck as he stared round-eyed at the men crowded around the exam table. Lillian pulled the boy closer as they both looked on.

The vet's gruff, "Let's get some X rays," sounded positive to Lillian, and she whispered to Joey, "Good. If the doctor wants X rays, it must mean there's hope."

The boy's voice was small as he whispered, "He can't die…"

Just then, Rye glanced back, saw them there and called out a low, "Go back to the waiting room. He'll do what he can."

Joey started to refuse, but Lillian got to her feet and gently led him away from the open door.

Once they reached the waiting room, which was mercifully empty, Joey walked to a sofa near the large aquarium that was mounted in the wall. Once he sat down, his brave little face crumpled and he turned away to press his forehead against the back of the sofa. His narrow shoulders shook with silent sobs.

The sight of the boy's grief gave her heart a forceful twist. Lillian sat down beside him. Though she was terrified she might be handling the situation wrong, she laid a gentle hand on his shoulder.

When he didn't shrug her off, Lillian moved closer and gave him an awkward pat. "They'll do all they can, sweetheart," she said, then caught her breath in surprise when the boy suddenly turned and threw himself against her. His arms found their way around her neck and he sobbed into her shoulder as if his heart were breaking.

Shocked that the sobbing child clung to her as if she somehow represented security to him, Lillian gently folded him in her arms. His straight golden brown hair was damp with sweat and smelled like sunshine and dirt. Untroubled by the fact that his hair was no longer clean and sleek, Lillian rested her cheek against his head, then shifted the boy into a more comfortable position against her.

In no time at all, the boy climbed completely onto her lap. When at last his tears had passed, the two of them sat quietly. Lillian toyed with a strand of the child's hair, amazed at the tender feelings she had for him.

Joey Parrish was a sweet little boy. Handsome, polite, well-behaved, he would make any parent proud. The reminder that his parents were dead was unbearably sad for Lillian. Especially since she knew firsthand how devastating the death of a parent was to a small child. At least she'd had a sister who'd gone through it all with her. Joey had no siblings.

The tragedy of it made her want to cry and she said a silent prayer, imploring God to let the pup live so the boy wouldn't have to suffer another loss.

Rye watched Lillian and Joey from the end of the hall. Joey was cuddled on Lillian's lap and they were both watching the fish swim lazily in the aquarium. They were so absorbed in watching the fish and talking that they were unaware of him.

"What was your dog's name?" Joey was asking.

A soft smile curved Lillian's lips and she replied, "Tootles."

Joey shifted and leaned back a bit so he could see her face. "Tootles?" He gave a snort that indicated how silly he thought the name was.

"Tootles. She was a Yorkshire terrier."

"What kind of dog is that?" was Joey's next question.

"A tiny dog with lots of hair, the kind of dog you put bows on and take to dog shows."

Lillian laughed softly when Joey made a face of boyish revulsion. "A sissy dog!"

"Of course. But I loved that sissy dog."

"Did you get to keep Tootles after your mom and dad died?"

Lillian looked uncomfortable but she smiled. Rye could tell the smile was forced. "No. My grandmother never got along with Tootles. She had to find a new home."

"Did you see Tootles after that?"

Rye saw Lillian swallow, then force another one of those stiff little smiles. "No. My grandmother thought it was best if I didn't know where she was."

Joey stared into her face as if he sensed she wasn't telling him everything, but Lillian went on.

"At least you'll know where Buster is when you go to live with your aunt. Your cousins will give him a good home at the ranch and you'll get to visit him sometimes."

Joey sighed and leaned against her to rest his head on her shoulder. "Yeah. But what if he doesn't make it?"

Lillian hugged him tighter for a few moments. "We can keep hoping. The vet is still working on him, so there must be hope."

The sight of Joey sitting on Lillian's lap, leaning against her while she held him in her arms and absently ran her fingers through his hair stirred peculiar emotions in Rye. Joey was all over dirt from the dog, and Lillian's clothes were now as filthy as Joey's. Tear trails had cut through dust smudges on both their faces, then dried to faint brown streaks, but neither of them appeared to notice.

Lillian didn't seem to care that she was dirty and mussed or that there was a dirty, mussed little boy on her lap. From the looks of things, neither of them had gone to wash up since they'd arrived, and that had been nearly an hour ago.

And to hear them talk! Cuddling together like a mother and son might, while Lillian told him about her childhood as if she were genuinely trying to help Joey with his.

Things Rye's mother had never done, never been capable of doing. Old yearnings began to stir but Rye ruthlessly ignored them. He was a man now. Man enough to see that the tenderness and affection Lillian lavished on his young cousin was cruel. Joey would naturally be vulnerable to the mothering of any woman, but when Lillian was destined to return to New York at any time, any attachment the boy formed to her would be disastrous.

Rye had to do something to thwart her thoughtlessness or Joey would have a whole new heartbreak to deal with.

"Joey?"

Rye's low, gruff voice startled them.

Joey and Lillian glanced his way, the sudden anxiety on their faces so remarkably alike that it jolted him. If he hadn't known better, he would swear he was looking at a mother and son.

"Don't get your hopes up too high," Rye warned, "but the vet thinks Buster has a good chance to pull through." The news brought identical reactions as they both smiled. Joey bounded to his feet and rushed to Rye. Lillian stood and followed at a calmer pace.

"Can we take him home now?" Joey burst out, the

eagerness on his small face underscoring the relief Rye felt at being able to give the boy good news.

He shook his head as he hunkered down and pulled the boy close for a rough hug. "The vet's still working on him. He'll need to stay here at least overnight. They'll be able to tell more in the morning."

Joey looked up at him. "Can I see him now?"

Rye shook his head. "The doc's not through with him yet. It'll be at least another hour. Meantime, why don't we get you cleaned up? We can get some ice cream down the street, then come back later."

"Ice cream?"

Rye nodded, then pointed the boy in the direction of the rest room. "As soon as we get you cleaned up."

Eager to have ice cream and see his dog, Joey dashed ahead to the bathroom as Rye stood up.

Lillian watched Joey go, a little ache in her heart as she felt the magic of the past hour dissipate. Rye turned and followed the boy. She heard the sound of water running as Joey chattered happily about his dog. Rye's low voice calmly ordered him to, "Stand still and lift your chin."

She suddenly could picture him trying to use a paper towel to wash the boy's face.

Joey's excited, "Should we wash my arms, too? Don't we need to keep germs away from Buster now? What about my clothes?" made her laugh softly. How had she not realized how wonderful children could be?

Rye and Joey emerged from the rest room. As if he'd just noticed Lillian also needed to clean up a bit, Joey told Rye, "We gotta wait for Lillian to wash her hands and face." Then to Lillian, "Hurry, Lillian."

The boy's thoughtfulness touched her heart. She

looked to Rye, saw his frown, but was drawn back to Joey when he pleaded, "Hurry, Lillian. We'll wait."

Lillian smiled at the boy. "I'll hurry," she assured him, then walked swiftly to the rest room and closed the door.

Her reflection in the mirror was a shock. She had never been so dusty and disheveled in all her life. She used a wad of paper towels to brush some of the loose dust from her clothes but, mindful of the boy's eagerness to leave so they could come back, she threw the towels away and got fresh ones. Once she used a bit of hand soap to wash her face, hands and arms, she quickly exited the rest room to join Rye and Joey in the hall.

Rye took Joey's hand, then led the boy down the hall to the door, leaving Lillian to follow. His obvious effort to keep her separated from the two of them reemphasized the notion that she was an intruder in their lives.

But once they all stepped out into the heat of late afternoon, Joey pulled Rye to a halt. He waited until Lillian caught up, then took her hand and tugged at Rye's. Joey was the only one who seemed thrilled when the three of them walked hand in hand down the sidewalk to the Dairy Queen.

CHAPTER SIX

SUPPER that night was tense. Now that he felt less inhibited by Lillian's presence, Joey chattered at the table, oblivious to the strain between her and his cousin. Even though he'd carried most of the conversation at the meal, the boy managed to clear his plate.

"Can I go play video games, Rye?" he asked.

Rye's, "Go ahead, but set the timer," made Joey give an aggrieved sigh. "That rule was Aunt Jenny's. Can't we make a new rule for here?"

Rye lifted his coffee cup for a sip, but Lillian caught a glimpse of the faint smile he concealed from the boy. "Add fifteen minutes, but for tonight only."

Joey sprang up from his chair and gave an energetic "Yippee! Thanks, Rye," then rushed from the room.

Now that Joey wasn't around to fill in the silence, it seemed to roar between them. Joey's presence had also been a protection of sorts. Once they heard a television go on in a distant room and the musical fanfare of a game cartridge begin, Rye leveled his gaze on her. He got straight to the point.

"I don't want you to cuddle and pet the boy like you did at the vet's today. And you don't need to give the impression that you're hanging on every word he says like he's the cutest kid you've ever laid eyes on, either."

Lillian stared over at his somber expression, shocked. "What are you talking about?"

"I'm talking about cuddling and crying and telling the boy sad little doggie stories," he growled, then threw his napkin down next to his plate as if he'd been disgusted by what he'd overheard.

A tide of hot color flooded Lillian's cheeks as Rye scraped back his chair and rose. She pulled her napkin off her lap with unsteady fingers and lifted it to the table.

"And now that we're finally alone, how the hell did Rocky run over the boy's dog without knowing she did?" he demanded next.

Lillian stared at the tight anger on his face as she struggled to recover. She shook her head. Her soft, "What's wrong with you?" slipped out.

Her question pricked his temper. "There's nothing wrong with me. What's wrong is you making over the boy, playing Mommy when you know you're going to walk out of his life forever the first chance you get."

Unable to remain sitting while Rye towered at the other end of the table, Lillian got shakily to her feet. "I think you're being unreasonable. The boy was distraught and you didn't come to the waiting room for nearly an hour. It would have been heartless not to comfort him."

Rye gave a grunt. "Kindness can be cruel."

Lillian shook her head. "I don't understand. You left a very upset child in my care, then you criticize me for taking care of him."

"But you didn't just take care of him, did you? No, you took him on your lap, cried over his dog with him, then told him a sad little story about yoursel—"

"What was wrong with that?"

He ignored the question. "I know your kind, lady. You've never had a thought or impulse in your life that wasn't centered on yourself somehow. It probably made you feel good to hold some kid and tell him about your petty little trials—maybe made you feel like more of a woman—but the boy took that little bit of mothering to heart. See how he's hung on to you since then and practically not let you out of his sight until a minute ago?" he demanded.

"And all because," he concluded harshly, "you didn't have a thought beyond what made *you* feel all warm and fuzzy. How do you think he's going to feel when you pack your bags and waltz outta here?"

Taken aback, Lillian couldn't speak for a moment. She nearly choked on the hysterical little laugh that bubbled up, but she smiled at him with an aplomb that was pure theater.

"It doesn't seem to be my day, does it?" she remarked brittlely. "On the other hand, it's really a shame that my sister didn't run off to marry you, Mr. Parrish. Particularly since the two of you seem to be the male and female sides of the same bent coin. I pity your brother having to suffer either of you. He seems quite civil."

Lillian watched as a dark flush crept along Rye's cheekbones. His blue eyes blazed at her as she stepped to the side and slid her chair up to the table.

"Did your sister know she ran down the dog?" he demanded again.

Lillian gave a faint shrug. "I didn't see it happen, but since Rachel sounded the horn, she probably saw the dog and was warning him out of the way." She sighed, resigned to what she had to tell him. "The car was smallish. If you hit a dog that large with it, you'd feel the impact and at least check your rearview mirror."

Rye's face was like stone. "So you're saying she knew she hit the dog, but didn't bother to stop."

"I'm saying exactly that, Mr. Parrish. Which is why I intend to take care of the vet bill for the dog if my sister wo—"

"The hell you will," he interrupted.

"The hell I won't," she retorted with soft defiance, uncomfortable with the profanity. "I feel badly about what she did. If your brother has any judgment that's not connected to his libido, then the bill, whatever it is, will be a bargain. It's just a shame poor Buster had to suffer."

Lillian went silent. She hated confrontations, but it seemed she was doomed to live in a world filled with angry, belligerent people. It was a shock to realize she'd stood up to Rye Parrish and survived—indeed had managed to handle herself well enough that he was silent now.

Furious, she noted, but silent. They stared at each other guardedly.

The past twenty-four hours had been one of the most traumatic segments of her adult life and she was exhausted. She wanted to leave, to find a quiet motel room somewhere, but she needed to be on hand should her sister return tonight. They both needed to be present tomorrow for Eugenia's call. Then, hopefully, Lillian could escape this barbaric place and go back to New York with her sister.

"I'll be in my room for the evening. I'd appreciate if you'd let me know when Rachel returns," she said, then turned and walked from the kitchen with rigid dignity.

Rye backed into the dim hall and pulled Joey's door closed. After the excitement of the day, the boy had fallen asleep before Rye had read halfway down a page of *Treasure Island*. Often the secret of getting Joey to sleep was to keep him motionless for a few moments. Making him lie quietly while he was being read to did the trick many nights. Even so, they'd managed to get through a substantial part of the classic tale this summer.

Once he walked down the hall to the living room, he heard the heavy tick-tock of the pendulum clock in the corner. Dovey had gone to his quarters in the east wing of the house hours before. He knew Lillian was still awake in her room because he'd seen a thin strip of light beneath the hall door.

It surprised him that she'd willingly sleep in that room again after waking up to find a dead snake in the bed. Perhaps their little go-round tonight and the one she'd had with her sister at lunch had toughened her up.

He crossed the room to the bar and selected a stout tumbler. He got a couple ice cubes from a bowl in the small refrigerator and tossed them into the glass. The decanter he selected held an inch of whiskey. He briefly debated getting out a new bottle, but settled on what was in the decanter.

Rye carried his drink to the darkened kitchen, then out to the patio. He stepped from beneath the roof overhang and looked up into the star-strewn sky overhead. Even with the lights around the headquarters, the stars were bright. On the range they would stretch from horizon to horizon and blaze so clear and seem so close that if you looked up into them long enough, you could feel the peculiar sensation of being drawn upward.

Rye wanted to be drawn somewhere tonight. He downed more of the whiskey, realized it was already running low, and wished he'd brought the new bottle with him. He thought he'd overcome the worst of his feelings about his mother and her abandonment, but he'd been wrong. His upset with Lillian that afternoon at the vet's office proved it.

Just thinking about her riled him, made him restless.

She stirred feelings in him that had nothing to do with his mother, dark feelings that were sensual and tender and dangerous. Feelings so strong they weakened him, just as they'd weakened his father and his brother.

But he'd be damned if he let those feelings destroy him. They'd destroyed his father, and if his brother didn't wake up, they'd destroy him, too—him and another generation of Parrish children.

The rattle of a doorknob interrupted his thoughts. He turned his head toward the sound and saw the gauzy drapes on Lillian's French door move. The click-click, click-click told him she was checking the lock on the door to make certain it was secure. After last night, she probably would.

The lights were still on in her room. They lit the ivory panels of the opaque drapes, and backlit her slim form so he could see her silhouette on them. He tossed the melting ice cubes away, then set the empty tumbler on a low table while he watched.

Lillian parted the drapes and leaned toward the glass to look up as if she were trying to see the night sky. There was enough reflected light from the drapes for him to see her face and witness her disappointment when she realized she couldn't see much from inside.

He looked from her to the sky. The cosmos stretched to eternity over Texas. He looked back at her door in time to see her cup her hands around her eyes and press against the glass to see past the overhang. She wanted to see the stars, but after her experience the night before, she probably wasn't brave enough to step outside and have a good, long look.

Watching her made his insides hum. The heavy warmth that he recognized as desire began to build and pulse low in his body. The arousal he'd experienced the night before came over him with slow force as he stood in the shadows watching her. Memories of what she'd felt like beneath him, of how satiny and warm her skin had been, moved through him like a molten flood.

Lillian released the edge of the gauzy drape and stepped away from the French doors. Rye watched her silhouette as she began to pace.

She hadn't changed for bed yet. She was still wearing the white blouse and khaki slacks she'd changed into before supper. He was disappointed she wasn't wearing another satin gown.

The memory of how she'd felt against him, how her small perfect breast had felt in his hand the night before, tortured him. Her lips had been petal soft and he'd not been able to get enough of their tender fullness or the sweetness of her mouth. Remembering it all made him crave more.

Lillian Renard could be a pleasant way to pass a summer night. The compulsion to prove she had no hold on him and never would, made the possibility of seducing her tantalizing. The desire he felt for her didn't mean anything, not really. He'd had women before, satisfied both them and himself, then had been able to walk away.

It would be no different with Lillian. These deep, disturbing feelings meant nothing.

As if Parrish family honor demanded he prove it, he walked to the French doors and stopped. He hesitated as he watched her silhouette through the drapes, then rapped a knuckle on a glass pane.

Her soft, "Who's there?" prompted him to answer.

"It's me."

"Is Rachel home?" she asked, the question telling him what she expected from him at this time of night.

"She's not back yet."

He let the silence stretch a moment, then said, "It's a clear night, no moon, the temperature's mild. If the notion appeals, you might want to see the night sky before you leave."

He saw her straighten and recognized the signal of interest. She took a step toward the door before she stopped.

"I'm a bit leery of...snakes. Is it safe to walk outside after dark?"

If her first thought was safety, then she wouldn't refuse to go because she objected to what he'd said to her at supper. He felt himself smile.

"Last night was unusual. Buster had to go a ways from the house to get his snake."

Her soft, "Oh," sounded noncommittal, but Rye sensed he'd lost her before she added, "Thank you. Maybe I'll take a walk...later."

Lillian winced at the silence that followed her small declaration. She couldn't have made it clearer that she didn't want to walk with *him*. His gruff, "Suit yourself," and the thud of his boot heels on stone told her he was walking away.

She instantly had second thoughts. What if his offer had been meant as a sort of olive branch? Lillian had never had many of those from her volatile sister or grandmother, so she wasn't certain.

Besides, Rye didn't have to be nice. He'd already proved he didn't feel obligated to be. Knowing that, his sudden offer to do something hospitable—to escort her on a walk so she could see the stars—might mean he'd softened toward her. If he'd decided to be a more gracious host, perhaps she should respond in kind.

Lillian reached out hesitantly, then unlocked the door and opened it.

"Rye?" She could see his tall outline only a few feet from the door. "I think I would like to see the stars now. Before it gets too late."

He stopped and turned toward her. His voice was a low smooth drawl. "Come on, then."

Lillian stepped out and closed the door quietly behind her. After the bright lights in the bedroom, the night was so dark that she was all but blind. She heard the soft scrape of his boot on a patio stone, then started when his fingers closed around her arm.

He gave her only a moment to adjust to the fact that he was touching her. Then he led her toward the far end of the patio, well away from the pool lights that gave the water a soft aqua glow. The only other light came from behind the drapes of her bedroom, and from a dim night-light in the kitchen. Lillian lagged back a bit, leery of moving too quickly over patio stones she could barely see.

His gruff, "What's wrong?" sounded strangely patient when he let her bring them both to a halt.

"I can't see very well yet."

"Your eyes haven't adjusted. Close 'em a few moments."

She hesitated, then dutifully closed them. She managed to slip her arm from his light grip and was relieved when he immediately released her. The feel of his calloused hand on her skin had been electric.

She sensed him ease away a step and she relaxed

more. After a moment, she opened her eyes and looked up.

"Oh, my..." she whispered as she stared at the star-studded blackness overhead. Slowly she turned, trying to take in the whole night sky.

"Know where the Big Dipper is?" Rye's deep voice was low, almost sensual.

Lillian searched the sky, then pointed up at the simple constellation. "There," she said softly, "with the Little Dipper and the North Star."

Rye watched Lillian's upturned face. He could make out her features in the shadowy light as she pointed out several constellations, her delight apparent as she enthusiastically rattled them off.

"I can't believe how bright they are here," she whispered, awed. "And *so, so many...*"

Lillian was so intent on the stars that she didn't realize those first moments how close Rye stood to her. Dizzy from looking up, she felt herself sway and put out a hand for balance. Her fingers touched Rye's chest and she gasped. "Oh—I'm—"

Rye put his hand over hers to press it against his shirt-front. Lillian turned her head and stared at his shadowed face in the dim starlight. He slid his other hand around her waist and drew her slowly to himself. The heat of his big body radiated through their clothing, but by the time he'd pulled her flush against him, his heat scorched her.

Lillian's knees went weak. "I—I'm sorry. Looking up sometimes makes me dizzy," she got out, then tried to gently push herself away from him.

But instead of releasing her, Rye tightened his arm. Lillian stared up at him, shocked when he leaned down.

Panicked that he might kiss her, she turned her face at the last second so his lips landed harmlessly on the side of her neck.

As if the tender flesh of her neck had been his intent, Rye nudged her hair aside and began to nip gently at her sensitive skin. A startled breath caught in her chest as the nips became nibbles, then large, hot bites that communicated a sexual aggression that made her knees give out.

The sensations that stormed through her were sharp and fiery. The feel of his large hand palming her breast turned her blood into something thick and sweet. Compelled by the pleasure he was giving her, Lillian pushed her hands up his chest to his wide shoulders and tried to kiss his cheek. Her lips fell on his hair, on his ear. By then her blood was pounding through her veins so violently that she thought her heart would burst.

Suddenly, she had to feel his mouth on hers. The craving to experience again the gloriously carnal kiss he'd pressed on her the night before made her the aggressor.

"Please," she whispered, the husky tremor in her voice sounding alien to her. "Please...I need...you." She slid her fingers into his hair and tightened them into fists. The gentle pressure she exerted guided him from her neck.

Rye lifted his head and his lips crashed forcefully against hers. At almost the same moment, his hand fell away from her breast. Lillian whimpered with disappointment, then nearly fainted when he leaned down to catch her behind the knees and lift her into his arms.

He broke the fiery kiss to growl, "Let's finish this inside."

Emotions Lillian couldn't identify blazed to life. Joy,

lust, terror and love churned in the mix, but she was already too senseless to sort them out. She kissed his jaw, his ear, his neck as he strode across the patio with her, too secure in the confidence he exuded to worry about a misstep.

Rye opened the patio door to his bedroom, then kicked it shut behind them. He stopped halfway to the bed to kiss her again, but this time his lips were more seductive than dominant, more persuasive than aggressive.

Lillian kissed him back, unaware that her lashes were damp with tears, or that there was something almost desperate about the way she was kissing him.

For her, his attention, his passion, validated her as a woman. He was telling her with his lips, with his body and with his sexuality that she was desirable, perhaps even lovable. The fact that he was a handsome, virile man somehow elevated her from the sexually repressed nonentity she had been, into a woman fully equipped with all that it took to draw a desirable male to herself.

The wonder of it—the sheer joy—made her heart soar. Lillian tightened her arms around his neck and tried to put everything she had into her part of the kiss.

It confused her when he withdrew a bit. Though his warm lips toyed with hers and lingered as if it was difficult for him to break the contact, she sensed this was the end, that the kisses would stop.

The notion that she'd disappointed him somehow—had she been too eager, not eager enough?—made her heartsick. Now she sensed the stillness in him, the terrible quiet that presaged storms of nature and storms of ire.

He slowly unbent his arm and let her legs slide down

until her feet touched the carpet. Lillian pulled her arms from around his neck and moved away the instant she was standing on her own. She stopped at arm's length from him in the dark room.

Her soft, "W-what's wrong?" trembled. She was suddenly terrified of what he'd say.

"Everything."

The word brutally summed up his feelings somehow, and sliced into her tender heart like a blade. She nodded, though the room was probably too dim for him to see. Shame sent fire across her cheeks.

"I understand. We met just a bit more than twenty-four hours ago. None of this is appropriate so soon."

"That's just it, honey," he said grimly. "If we get into that bed, it'll be sex to me. To you, it'll mean a society wedding and a 15-karat diamond ring through my nose. But then, you'd equate sex with a marriage proposal no matter when it happens—twenty-four hours after we meet, or twenty-four months."

Lillian stared at his shadowy form, surprised at how keen his perception was—but stunned at how opposite their expectations were.

"So," he went on, "unless you're willing to climb into that bed and have sex with a man who won't remember what you look like a week after you're gone, you'd better go back to your room."

The silence between them was harsh. The invisible wall between them was truly impenetrable.

Lillian was crushed. The disappointment she felt humiliated her almost as much as her wanton behavior moments ago shamed her now.

She'd been about to get naked with a man who had no regard for her. She'd been so unexpectedly starved for the romantic attentions of any man that she'd almost had sex with the first one who'd touched her.

The knowledge that he could've slept with her that night, then coldly ignored her the next morning made her ill. She had no doubt he really would forget what she looked like, but she was certain it would take him much less than a week to do so.

Lillian stood stiffly, smarting from the hurt and the shame she'd brought on herself. She had to recover somehow, had to seize at least a scrap of the dignity she'd thrown away.

"Thank you for clearing things up, Mr. Parrish," she said quietly. "I think I will go back to my room. Good night."

Feeling so awkward she was barely coordinated enough to move, she managed to turn from him and walk calmly to the door that connected their rooms. Even in the dark, she could feel his gaze follow her every move.

Once she stepped into her room and closed the door, she sagged weakly against it. Suddenly she knew how a wee mouse felt when it escaped the jaws of a hungry lion. The analogy was so accurate that she shivered.

He'd meant to seduce her. One time with the little socialite from New York would have put out the fire and proved he was immune to her.

The problem was that Lillian was obviously a virgin. Her inexperience touched him, partly because it was so unexpected in any sister of Rocky's, and partly because he sensed she'd never had a choice in the matter. He could picture Rocky enticing romantic prospects away from the painfully reserved, ladylike Lillian. Rocky had made a nasty remark that afternoon about Lillian's inability to meet men, so perhaps she'd never had any suitors.

It wouldn't be fair to seduce a woman like that, then later rebuff her. Not even if the woman was an exact copy of his coldhearted mother.

Rye got ready to turn in. He laid awake a long time as he tried to remember all the ways Lillian reminded him of his mother. To his surprise, it wasn't Lillian, but her sister, Rocky, who reminded him most of Rena Parrish.

CHAPTER SEVEN

LILLIAN didn't sleep well that night. Her romantic disaster with Rye kept her tossing in bed through the night, mentally reliving each thrilling second with him under the stars, then replaying the agonizing moments that followed when he'd suddenly rejected her.

It still shocked her to think he could kiss her like that, goad her toward such mindlessness, then as much as tell her she meant nothing to him and never would. For a man who'd claimed he wouldn't remember what she looked like in a week, he'd shown surprising consideration in letting her know the score ahead of time.

The memory of how close she'd come to giving herself to him made her insides twist. The man was a virtual stranger and a rude, ungracious host. How could she have responded to him like that?

At seven a.m., Lillian finally dragged out of bed and dressed for the day. It didn't surprise her that she was still trying to figure things out. Why had she responded to Rye the way she had? Was she that starved for affection?

On the other hand, she'd never experienced such a strong attraction to any man. He was not only worlds different from the mild-mannered cultured men she'd been exposed to all her life, he was their antithesis.

Was she attracted to him because he was so different, so macho and abrasive and arrogant? As she carefully applied her makeup and brushed her hair, she realized that machismo, abrasiveness and arrogance were not necessarily negative traits to her. Coming from the family she did, no pleasant, easygoing man was likely to make much of an impression on her, much less have the go-to-hell attitude he'd need to stand up to Eugenia.

Lillian stared grimly at her reflection. Just thinking about her formidable grandmother awakened the sense of doom she'd felt during her call the day before. Eugenia had fumed for weeks over Rachel's wedding plans, but now that Rachel was refusing to go home and had disclosed information about Lillian's real mother, Eugenia's temper must be white-hot. Hadn't she heard it herself in her grandmother's voice yesterday, sensed it in her curt order to be on hand for her call today?

Instead of trying to analyze the reasons for her intense attraction to Rye, she should have been thinking more about what Rachel had said about the circumstances of her birth. On the other hand, she wasn't certain she wanted to think much about it yet, not when Eugenia hadn't immediately confirmed the information.

It would be a relief to think that Margaret Renard's inability to love her hadn't been because she'd been an unlovable child. If it really was true that Margaret had been forced to accept another woman's child—a child of her husband's infidelity—and pass it off as her own, it would explain much of Lillian's unhappy childhood. Margaret's coldness and neglect, her father's attempts to compensate, Eugenia's extreme favoritism toward the legitimate child of the woman she'd insisted her only son marry...

The small tap-tap-tap she heard at the hall door interrupted her thoughts. She gave her hair a last brushing, then stepped over to the door and called out a quiet, "Yes?"

Joey's voice was a loud whisper. "Are you awake, Miz Lilly?"

Her heart ached a bit at the hopefulness in his voice. How did Rye expect her to keep clear of the boy when they were both guests in the same house? Unable to believe anyone could truly become emotionally attached to her in such a brief time, Lillian turned the knob and pulled the door open.

"Awake and ready for breakfast," she declared with pleasant cheer. "Have you eaten?"

Joey grinned up at her. "Yeah, I ate with Rye, but I can have a doughnut with you while you eat."

"What kind of doughnut?"

"The kind that'll make us fat and clog our otteries, Aunt Jenny says."

Lillian giggled at the otteries and reached out to touch Joey's shoulder fondly. "Ah, the good kind, then," she said with a smile before she stepped out to walk with Joey to the kitchen.

How could she ignore this child? As the two of them walked side by side down the hall, Joey chattered to her, mostly about the various beds he was planning to make around the house for Buster while he recuperated.

Clearly, he missed having some sort of female attention in his life. It had nothing to do with fixating on her as a mother figure and becoming dangerously attached.

The two of them had a peaceful breakfast together. Lillian learned from Dovey that while Chad had come home in the wee hours that morning, Rachel had yet to return to the ranch or to even call. Dovey suggested Rachel might have checked into a motel in town, since she'd done that before. He then offered to set out the local telephone directory in the den if she wanted to make a few calls to check.

What Lillian secretly hoped was that her unpredictable sister had gone to the airport and bought a ticket back to New York. Rachel had gone over the line yesterday when she'd run down Buster then driven away. Surely she knew that. It would be quite in character for her to race back to the sanctuary of Eugenia's domain to escape the consequences. It would also simplify things for everyone else.

Her first call after breakfast was to the ticket counter of the local airport. No Rachel or Rocky Renard had made a reservation or bought a ticket that morning or the day before. Lillian was able to check quickly with the registration desks of the six hotels and motels that Dovey indicated were within a reasonable distance from the ranch. None of the six listed Rachel's name.

By the time she finished with her calls, Lillian was worried. Rachel liked living recklessly and believed she could handle herself in any situation. That was precisely why Lillian thought Rachel was at such risk. Crimes against women were frequent and violent these days, but Rachel didn't seem to care.

Lillian leaned back in the heavy leather and wood swivel chair behind Rye's desk and tried to think where her sister might be. Had she made friends in the area?

It startled her when the telephone rang. Dovey must have caught it, because it quit ringing in the middle of the second ring. Lillian stood up, closed the thin phone book, then set it neatly beside the desk blotter. She walked around the desk and was halfway to the door when she heard Dovey call her on the intercom.

"Phone's for you, Miz Lillian. Long distance from your grandma."

Lillian hurried to the desk, briefly examined the intercom, then pressed the reply button. "Thank you,

Dovey.'' She picked up the telephone receiver, anxiety pulsing through her. Eugenia's call had come earlier than she'd expected, and Rachel wasn't here. The fact that Lillian had no idea where her sister was compounded the problem.

"Good morning, Grandmama," she began, striving to keep her voice as calm and pleasant as possible.

Eugenia's voice was brittle. "Where's Rachel?"

It was inevitable that her first concern would be Rachel. Lillian ignored the prick of disappointment.

"As I told you yesterday, Rachel was quite upset by my arrival. She left the ranch after I spoke with you and she hasn't returned yet." Lillian didn't tell Eugenia that Rachel had seriously injured Joey's dog. Her grandmother would consider such information unimportant.

"Where is she?" Eugenia demanded.

Lillian pressed trembling fingers to her temple. Eugenia would be furious. "No one seems to know. I checked the hotels and motels in the area. However, the Parrishes are well-known here. I'm certain if anything were amiss they'd be notified immediately."

Though she didn't know this for a fact, she assumed it was true. The Parrish brothers had to be at least as influential in their part of the world as Eugenia Renard was in hers. "I also checked with the ticket counter at the airport in case she'd decided to come home to you. That's always a possibility," she added carefully.

The silence from her grandmother's end of the line weighed heavily on her.

When Eugenia finally spoke, her voice was cold. "So you did handle the situation poorly yesterday. As a result, everything has become much worse, particularly since Rachel is missing."

Lillian felt the criticism like a slap. "I'm sorry,

Grandmama,'' she got out, the words bitter in her mouth. "Rachel resents me, I'm afraid. It might have been better to send someone else."

"It wasn't possible to send anyone else," Eugenia asserted. "Not when young Rachel needs a graphic lesson to demonstrate the importance of respecting her inheritance. She doesn't realize how crucial it is that she not jeopardize the privileged lifestyle she so enjoys. After all, the world is a cruel, dismal place."

Lillian's heart did a free fall. She sensed what was coming, felt it roaring toward her with a suddenness that stole her breath and made her heart pound. Eugenia went on as if she were dictating a letter to a stranger.

"And so, I believe Rachel will rapidly come to her senses once she sees how difficult it is for you to be without money or resources."

Lillian's soft, "Grandmama?" was barely audible. Eugenia went on.

"As of this morning, you will no longer enjoy my support, financial or otherwise."

The calm declaration made Lillian's heart jump. As if she were indifferent to the trauma she was dealing her granddaughter, Eugenia continued.

"I've canceled your credit cards and closed your bank accounts. Your stocks and investments have been transferred. In short, you have no assets of any real value available to you until your twenty-fifth birthday. At that time, the trust fund your father set up for you will be yours.

"Your personal belongings are yours, of course, including your better jewelry, as well as whatever cash or traveler's checks you might have with you there now. In a few days, I'll wire you five hundred dollars. That should be enough to buy a plane ticket somewhere.

Perhaps you have some friends you can visit for an in-definite period. Then, if I were you, I'd make finding a husband a priority, since it will be two long years until you turn twenty-five."

The world was spinning. Lillian could barely stand. She grabbed for the edge of the desk and gripped it tightly. Eugenia's cultured voice went on relentlessly.

"However, should your sister break her engagement and return to New York, your situation could improve. But I warn you, the longer she stays in Texas, the less inclined I shall be to be generous with you."

Lillian managed to sit down in the big chair behind the desk. Feeling faint, she tried to calm her pounding heart. The terror she felt made her nauseous.

"Until then, you're on your own, just as Rachel will be if she persists with this nonsense. My investigator will make this clear when he visits her motel. By the way," Eugenia added, "your sister registered under the very unimaginative name of Smythe, which explains why you weren't able to find her."

Lillian squeezed her eyes closed. Eugenia had known all along exactly where her favorite was. The bitter thought, *You should have known*, went through her mind. The hurt she felt was so overwhelming she almost couldn't bear it those next moments.

Eugenia's brisk, "Lillian—are you there?" brought her back. "Unless I hear from you regarding a destina-tion, I'll have your things sent—"

"Is what Rachel said about my mother true?" she interrupted. Eugenia was about to end the conversation. End it just as suddenly as she'd ended what little security Lillian had ever been sure of. She couldn't let her hang up before she had an answer. "Surely you could spare me a few answers before..." Her voice trailed off as emotion overwhelmed her.

There was silence, but it was charged, angry. "Your father had an affair with a worthless little shop girl the first year he was married to Margaret. I bought her off, but she took the money, delivered you to your father and stayed in New York only long enough to have a judge terminate her parental rights. Once the legalities were out of the way, your father insisted on bringing you into our lives. He presented you to Margaret and I, delivered his ultimatum, and upset poor Margaret so much that she lost the baby she was carrying. Of course, that made it possible for us to pass you off as Margaret's, since you were rather small."

"W-what was my mother's name?" she got out.

"It hardly matters now, Lillian," she said crisply. "She had no family and she passed away some time ago."

Eugenia paused to signal the change of subject, but Lillian had heard enough. She pulled the phone from her ear and leaned forward to place the receiver quietly in its cradle.

That done, she braced her elbows on the desk and pressed her forehead against her palms. Her head was spinning, and she was sick from head to toe.

What would she do? How would she live? It shamed her that she was so ill prepared to be on her own. It crushed her to know that her only real value to her grandmother was as an object lesson to her sister.

At that moment, Lillian felt like the most insignificant and terrified, desperate and lonely human on the planet.

Eventually, her brain started functioning again. She had to do something, had to make some sort of plan. She got up shakily and hurried to her room for her handbag. She dumped its contents on the bed, then checked her wallet for the cash she'd brought with her. The long sleeve of credit cards was useless, but she had three hundred dollars in traveler's checks stashed in a zippered compartment. With the five hundred dollars Eugenia would send in a few days and the cash she had left, she'd have a bit less than a thousand dollars.

A thousand dollars. An amount that wouldn't last longer than a few days, if that long, for food and shelter in New York. Fortunately, other places were less expensive to live in. Surely small-town Texas was one of those places. With careful management, a thousand dollars might last weeks.

She carried her wallet back to the den. She opened the telephone book, then phoned the motels she'd called earlier and asked about their rates. She chose one of the less expensive ones and made a reservation. The motel wouldn't need to know that the credit card number she'd given them to secure the room had been canceled, since she'd be paying for the room with cash.

That done, she made her way back to her room to pack. She was beginning to feel a bit better, but her hands shook as she dragged her suitcases out of the closet. The bottle of rare vintage cognac she'd brought as a thank-you gift for her hosts still rested in the wooden box she'd had wrapped in bright blue foil. All that was left was to attach the bow and ribbon streamers she'd brought along and to write out the personal thank-you-for-your-hospitality note she always left when she was an overnight guest in someone's home.

Lillian sat down to write a practice note, dismayed that her handwriting was barely legible. Tears stung her eyes, but she refused to let them fall. She wouldn't cry, not now.

There was too much to do.

It was barely ten a.m. by the time she'd packed everything and finished with the gift and note. She was about to lug her suitcases to the front door when she was startled by a tap on the glass of the French door.

Because she'd opened the drapes before breakfast that morning to enjoy the view of the patio, anyone walking close enough to the door would be able to see in. Her brain had been so fogged with shock and frantic plans when she'd come back, that she'd not given the drapes a thought.

Now Rye stood at the door, his harsh gaze taking in the suitcases on the bed. Lillian stared over at him, not surprised when he opened the door and walked in without waiting for her to grant permission.

Without a word to her, he walked to the dresser where she'd left the foil wrapped thank-you gift and note. He picked up the note, read it, then tossed it casually to the dresser top. He looked over at her, his eyes meeting hers with an intensity that made her feel as if he could see into her soul.

"So you're leaving?"

Lillian stood so tensely that her entire body ached. "Y-yes. As a matter of fact. My gr—Eugenia called. Rachel is staying at a motel in town. I managed to make a reservation, and now I...need a ride. If you could spare someone to drive me."

"Does this mean the engagement's off?" Though his face was stern, the faint glint in his eyes betrayed his hope.

Lillian shook her head. "I don't know yet." She shrugged. "Though I don't see how it can last much longer. Rachel will be disowned if she goes through with the marriage. I'm not certain she'll risk it. Besides, your brother really isn't the man for her—not that there's anything wrong with him—he seems nice."

Lillian stopped and bit her tongue. Now she was babbling. Rye's gaze narrowed on her.

"What's in the box?"

"Cognac. I forget which brand."

His eyes moved over her face as if he'd seen something and was trying to decide what it was. "I'm obliged."

Lillian's nerves were screaming. "Thank you for letting me stay."

They were making small talk now and still his eyes were riveted to her, staring at her as if he suspected something, taking note of her clenched hands, the faint tremor of her lower lip before he drawled, "You ready to leave?"

She nodded, then used the excuse to look away from him. Feeling the debilitating awkwardness that come over her at difficult times, she moved stiltedly to the bed and selected a suitcase. She got the medium-size one and turned with it.

But Rye was suddenly there and took it from her. "Get your handbag and the small case, if you want."

With that, he leaned past her to gather up the rest, forcing her to step out of his way or have him brush against her. She got the small bag and her purse, then hurried ahead of him to get the door. When they reached the front door, she opened it, but he called her to a halt.

"Better go tell Dovey and the boy you're leaving. Chad's not around now, but they're on the patio."

The reminder that it was simple courtesy to tell them each goodbye shamed her a little. She wasn't thinking straight enough to observe that bit of good manners, but it should have come automatically.

"Of course. I'll just be a minute." She set down her case and her handbag then turned to head to the kitchen. Once there, she let herself out the patio door.

Dovey and Joey were shucking large ears of sweet corn. When they heard the door swish open, they both looked her way.

"Hi, Lilly," Joey called. "Do ya like corn on the cob?"

Lillian made herself smile and hoped neither the boy nor Dovey gave her one of those see-all-the-way-to-your-soul looks Rye had given her.

"I don't eat corn on the cob often," she told the boy, using his words. In fact, she'd only eaten corn that way once in her life, but not in any of Eugenia's households.

Eugenia considered eating corn off the cob something a field hand would do.

"Then you're in for a treat, Miz Lillian," Dovey put in, compounding Lillian's guilt about leaving so abruptly.

She shook her head with real regret. "I'm sure I would be, Dovey, since your cooking is wonderful. But I need to leave this morning."

Dovey gave her a knowing look and nodded. "I figured your grandma's call was an important one."

Lillian felt her eyes smart at that. "It was. I wanted to thank you for your hospitality and compliment you again on your cooking. It was wonderful."

She glanced immediately at Joey, who stood silently watching her. "And I enjoyed having breakfast with you this morning, Joey. I'm sorry I won't be here to see Buster when he comes home, but I'm certain he'll recover nicely. You'll take good care of him until he's better, won't you?''

Oh, God—the look on his face when he said, ''Yeah. Goodbye, Miss Lilly,'' was a fresh nick on her wounded heart.

''Goodbye, Joey.'' She made herself look at Dovey and nod her goodbye to him because she suddenly couldn't speak. She turned and made a hasty escape into the kitchen and straight through the house to the front door.

Once there, she paused before going out to compose herself. Her small suitcase and handbag were no longer at the door, so she had no excuse to linger before she walked out and pulled the door closed behind her.

Rye drove her to the motel she'd indicated and waited in his car while she went into the office to register and get a room key. Rachel would never take a room in a budget motel like this one. Though she wanted Rye to believe she was meeting her sister at a motel, she knew if he thought about it at all, he'd realize Rachel would never come to this motel.

That she'd succeeded seemed evident when he didn't remark about her choice as he carried her things into her room.

She began to think he'd guessed nothing. Until he turned toward her. Suspicion drew his dark brows together slightly and his gaze was more intense than ever.

''Thank you for bringing me to town,'' she said quietly, then edged slightly away from the door in a silent signal for him to leave.

''Where's Rachel?''

The gruff question sent a shiver through her. She made herself shrug. ''Who knows? She has a car and she's never been one to sit around quietly. I'm certain I'll see her soon.''

Rye came toward her slowly. The glittering look in his eyes riveted her. He'd guessed something, she could see it. She glanced away, trying to conceal her panic.

She couldn't bear for him to know she'd been disowned. Not yet. Though he'd find out about it eventually, she didn't want him to guess now. She didn't want anyone's pity, and she absolutely couldn't stand for him to think she expected him to do anything for her just because she'd been in his vicinity when disaster struck.

She waited till the last possible moment—the moment when he stopped in front of her—before she glanced up at him and thrust out her hand for a handshake.

''Again,'' she said with as bright a smile as she could manage, ''thank you for allowing me to visit your home and thank you for driving me to town, carrying in my things—all that.'' Lillian clamped her lips together before she could babble more. She was nearly hysterical. Pain and fear and heartbreak were suddenly exploding in her as she looked up at him.

The sudden impression that Rye Parrish represented safety to her made her ache. She was more terrified than she'd ever been in her life; she was shaken to the core and grief-stricken about the tawdry circumstances of her birth and the rejection of her family, but she couldn't let herself reach out for this man.

Though the compulsion to seek the comfort and protection of another human being was so strong she could barely contain herself, she didn't dare seek it from Rye.

But then, perhaps he wouldn't pity her at all. Perhaps it was more in character for him to either scorn her or be amused at her predicament. In the end, she realized he'd made too many negative comments about her "kind" for her to take the risk.

The feel of her small, cold hand suddenly enveloped in the calloused heat of his gave her a start. She was so rattled she'd already forgotten she'd offered it for a handshake. She tried to draw back, but his free hand settled over the back of hers and pressed gently.

He leaned toward her. Lillian stood stiffly, disbelief keeping her eyes wide and fixed on his face until she felt his breath on her lips and his features blurred. Her lashes dropped closed as his mouth eased gently onto hers.

Too soon he pulled back, and she swayed toward him before she could catch herself.

"Goodbye, Lilly," he said, his drawl low and rough and tantalizing. "Don't come back to Texas."

And then he was gone, brushing past her to exit the room before she could get a breath. The sound of the door swinging shut behind him was jarring.

God help her, she stepped to the window and watched him go, not able to tear her eyes away until he'd got in his car and driven out of the parking lot. He was out of sight a full minute before Lillian could bring herself to turn away.

CHAPTER EIGHT

LILLIAN couldn't let herself think about her predicament beyond forming some sort of plan to survive. As soon as she'd unpacked a few clothes that might wrinkle, she stepped out of her room into the oppressive heat. She went to the newspaper vendor outside the motel office to buy a paper and took it back to her room to search the job ads.

She had no idea what she could do for a living, since she'd never supported herself. She could use a computer and was a fair typist, but she had no other office skills and no experience. She'd done some volunteer work, but it amounted to serving on boards and committees to organize charitable functions. How she could translate any of that into a job she could support herself with was a mystery.

The job ads filled two and a half columns in the thin daily, but most of those were agricultural jobs. She circled a handful of possibilities, then scanned the next page for apartments and rooms for rent. There weren't many choices there, either.

Hoping for leads on other jobs, she searched the drawers in the room for a telephone book, then turned to the Yellow Pages. By late afternoon, she'd begun making telephone calls.

It was seven in the evening before worry and restlessness drove her from her room. The air had cooled dramatically. Though it was past time to eat, she wasn't hungry. The sun wouldn't set for another two hours, so she decided a walk through the small town might relax her a bit and help her get her bearings.

Tomorrow, she'd find a job and a place to stay. If not tomorrow, then the next day. She did her best to keep calm, to be optimistic. Every day people found jobs, rented apartments and made a life for themselves.

She could, too. She had to.

It was as if she were jinxed.

During the next three days, Lillian applied for jobs at four businesses downtown and interviewed for two openings. She'd walked to the highway east of town to the Wal-Mart and filled out an application, but they wouldn't be interviewing for another week. She applied for waitress jobs at every restaurant and diner she passed, including the ice cream shop, but none were hiring. She applied at one of the two banks in town, but there were no openings there, either.

By end of the fourth day, she was worried sick. Even budget motels cost money. Eugenia had yet to wire her the five hundred dollars, although she'd called the local Western Union office twice a day to check. Meanwhile, she applied for jobs at the three motels in town, including the one she was staying at, but had no luck.

Today was Friday, the last day of the workweek. If she didn't find something today, she'd have to wait the whole weekend before she could look again. She went to the newspaper vendor outside the motel office at seven a.m. to buy the latest paper and hurry back to her room with it.

Her heart fell when she saw there were no new jobs listed. She'd already applied for every job on the page that wasn't agricultural. Except one.

Wanted: Gals to serve suds, snacks and smiles at pop-
ular Nightclub/Honky-tonk. It helps if you're gorgeous, but we'll like you fine if you're honest, hard-
working and polite to the customers. Come talk to
Roy or Louise at Uncle Pepper's Country Music
Revue, afternoons any day.

A honky-tonk. As far as she knew, a honky-tonk was a
disreputable bar with a reputation for drunken fights and
police raids. Most women would never go into a place
like that, much less take a job there.

Besides, the job was too public. Rachel frequented
bars. Perhaps Rye and Chad did, too. The shame she felt
at being disowned would be that much sharper if any of
them knew she had been reduced to taking a job in such
a place.

She braced her forehead on her hands and stared down
at the ad. No one else had hired her. Truth to tell, as an
outsider in town who, at the age of twenty-three, had
never held a job, she might not be considered a desirable
prospect by any employer.

*Should your sister break her engagement and return
to New York, your situation could improve...the longer
she stays in Texas, the less inclined I shall be to be
generous with you... Your father had an affair with a
worthless little shop girl...*

Lillian struggled for several moments as the shock and
heartbreak impacted her again. Eugenia had made her
feelings brutally clear. She not only wanted to use Lillian
to bring Rachel into line, she wanted to vent her outrage
on the grandchild who'd been forced upon her all those
years ago. A woman who'd held a grudge that many
years against someone who'd entered her life as a helpless infant would never relent.

Lillian forced herself to reread the ad. Pride was for people who had money. Though she'd have access to her trust fund in two more years, she had less than three hundred dollars now. Because she no longer believed Eugenia would send her the five hundred she'd promised, she'd be out of money long before she'd got her first paycheck.

Desperation helped her to decide. She'd seen Uncle Pepper's on the highway. It was a large, well-maintained building with a second story on the older half of the structure. The Las Vegas-style marquee over the newer half boasted, Smokey Rose Live This Friday and Saturday Night. Not only was the building one of the largest in or near town, but the graveled parking lot was huge. Maybe it wasn't as bad as all that.

The good part about working nights there was that she'd have weekdays free to look for something better. Also, if Uncle Pepper's had a large clientele that tipped even half as well as those in the Renard's social circle, perhaps she could earn more than minimum wage.

Lillian eventually got out the Yellow Pages and went through them again in search of a job possibility she might have overlooked. By noon, she fully accepted that she had no choice. It was a long, hot walk to the highway.

Rye finished with paperwork by six. Joey was at the neighbor's house, staying all night with the neighbor kids, so this was one Saturday night that was all his. The shrill feminine voice that drifted in from the patio sent a flash of bad temper through him.

"You know I hate that damned cowboy 'yup' and 'nope' way of talking." Rocky was saying.

Rocky had returned to the ranch the day after he'd

taken Lillian to town. She'd pretended not to have known she'd run down Buster. When Chad confronted her for lying, she'd turned on a veritable fountain of tears and bawled her way back into his good graces.

They'd been fighting ever since. And when they weren't fighting, Rocky seemed hell-bent to drag Chad from his work and force him to pay attention to her. Fortunately, Chad was rapidly growing tired of it all.

It wouldn't be long before Rocky was out of their lives for good. Though he'd thought that before, things had gotten worse the past few days. He didn't know why Rocky hung around. She hated the ranch, she hated the distance from "culture" and "civilization"—words and concepts that sounded odd coming from a woman who delighted in bad language and vulgarities.

The fact that she and Lillian were only half sisters explained many of the stunning differences between them.

As if his emotions had been waiting for that one mental slip, thoughts of Lillian flooded his mind. He could still taste the softness of her lips when he'd kissed her goodbye, could still feel the tremor of feminine vulnerability as he'd pressed her hand between his.

And her eyes. So huge and blue and tragic that day.

He'd closed his mind to the reasons for such tragedy. She couldn't have seen leaving the Parrish Ranch as a tragedy. Hell, for her, staying at the ranch had to have been one long nightmare. And he'd been terrible to her, critical one moment, unable to keep his hands off her the next.

Though he'd sensed something was wrong the day he'd taken Lillian to town, he'd left her there anyway. After all, what was tragedy to a woman who'd been pampered and spoiled all her life? Though she'd turned out to be quite different than he'd expected, she'd been born to a certain lifestyle and was possessed of a certain set of values. A lifestyle and set of values that were nothing like his own.

By now, Lillian would be back in New York, back to living the useless, ornamental, self-centered life of her kind. He'd been harsh with her, telling her not to come back to Texas, but he'd meant it. Texas was no place for her, and he didn't want her here.

The secret declaration shamed him a bit. He didn't want her here because she was a temptation.

Impatient with himself, he shoved away from the desk and stood. He hadn't been to Uncle Pepper's for weeks. Maybe he needed to get out more, take a serious turn at finding a special lady.

Though he didn't normally look for wife material in bars, Uncle Pepper's was different. It was the only decent place where singles could meet for a hundred miles in any direction, and it was the best place for live country bands and dancing. Everyone went to Uncle Pepper's, and everyone had a good time.

The way things had been going lately, he could use a good time. If it was an especially good night, he might meet someone. And if she was any kind of lady, she'd help him forget about Lillian Renard in the time it took to ask her to dance.

"Now you're gettin' it, Lil!"

Louise Pepper, the co-owner of Uncle Pepper's, gave her a grin and a thumbs-up as she shouted to be heard over the loud country music band.

Lillian gave her boss a quick smile, but the lion's share of her attention was on the tray of drinks she balanced as she moved away from the bar and made her way through the huge crowd. The table that was her destination seemed miles away.

Because she was new, she'd been assigned the worst section of tables and booths—the ones farthest from the kitchen and the bar. Because she was inexperienced, two of the other servers were helping her cover her area so service wouldn't be too lacking.

Lillian was frustrated by her slowness, frustrated by her ignorance of the items and prices on the food and drink menus, and frustrated that the band was so loud she had trouble hearing customer orders. Louise assured her that she would learn to read lips and that she'd have the menus memorized soon enough.

Meanwhile, the size of the crowd made her head spin. At times, the human congestion between booths and tables made it difficult to navigate with a tray. If she hadn't come early to work the day before just to spend time familiarizing herself with the floor plan of the large nightclub, she'd have been lost in the crowd the first night.

She'd taken the menus with her when she'd left work Friday night and had tried memorizing them. But the minute she'd got to work just before six this evening, Louise had informed her of a couple of price changes. She'd also added three new food items. Lillian had already undercharged a customer twice that evening. An undercharge she'd had to make up out of her own pocket.

At last, she made it to her destination. She forced a smile and lowered the tray to the table. Setting the right drink in front of each the three couples at the table was the one thing she'd managed to get consistently right all evening. She quickly took their money and made change, then thanked them when each of the couples passed her a tip.

Encouraged by the growing number of dollar bills in the pocket of the tight jeans she'd been given, she turned and took an order from the people at the two small tables nearby before she rushed back to the bar.

Rye watched the blonde on the other side of the room. A couple of his friends had pointed her out as the new girl. The band, Smoky Rose, was playing and the place was packed. There was so much smoke and distance and crowd between where she was and where he was, that he couldn't see her well enough to form an opinion.

He'd get a closer look later. Right now, Sheila Barnett, one of the prettiest single women around, was sitting nearby at a table of her girlfriends. She was a schoolteacher and a rancher's daughter, born to the life he loved, raised on the same values he'd been raised on. Sheila was perfect for him.

But as he made his way to her table and asked her to dance, he suddenly felt let down. By the time he led her to the dance floor and pulled her into his arms, he'd already lost interest. It aggravated him to realize how much more he suddenly preferred blondes. Reserved little blondes who weren't half as sure of their sex appeal as the tall, saucy brunette who snuggled up to him with a familiarity that put him off.

Uncle Pepper's crowd began to thin out after midnight. Rye managed to get a spare seat with some single friends at a booth in the blonde's territory. Though he was now much closer, whenever he caught glimpses of her, her back was always toward him.

So he enjoyed her backside. She was petite, and the

tight blue jeans and bright red tailored shirt that she and the other girls wore with their shirttails tied above their waists showed off her shapely little figure.

Yet in spite of the casual sexiness of the clothes, she carried herself like a royal, her head erect, her posture faultless. She moved with the grace and precise dignity of a charm school graduate, but the few strands of fine gold that had escaped the silver barrette on top of her head suggested a soft, approachable femininity that captured his attention. And reminded him of Lillian.

Impatient with himself, he was about to look away when she suddenly turned her head and showed her profile. The shock he felt was like a punch to the gut.

He didn't realize he'd half got to his feet to see better until one of his friends yelled across the table, "Lookin' at that new little gal? Name's Lilly."

Rye looked away from the blonde and glanced over at his friend. "What?"

Will leaned across the table and tried to yell over the band. "Lilly. From New York City. She don't know what she's doin' yet, but we already voted to forgive her, since she's so pretty 'n' sweet."

Rye realized he was glaring at his friend and managed to blank his expression and sit down.

Will nodded in Lillian's direction and Rye looked toward her. "Here she comes now. Catch her and I'll buy us another round."

Rye stared as Lillian made her way past the row of booths. She was wearing flashy silver and turquoise earrings that dangled enticingly from her ears. Her face was perfectly made up, but nothing like the softer, classier look she'd worn before.

Now, he noted with disapproval, her lashes were thick with dark mascara. Her eye shadow was blue and twinkled faintly like fine glitter. She wore blusher and her lipstick was as red as her blouse, emphasizing the soft shape of her mouth. She looked older now, definitely sexier, maybe a little cheap—and he was suddenly, inexplicably furious.

He didn't realize he'd caught her wrist as she passed, until she stopped abruptly and her blue eyes swung down to meet his. It was then that he noticed the fatigue that glazed her eyes, the weary surprise as he watched her recognize him. The blush that deepened the artificial color on her cheeks was heavy in the low light.

She tried to pull her wrist back, but he didn't let go. Instead, he eased her closer, all the while staring at her, chronicling the changes.

Lillian was first startled, then mortified. This was the moment she'd dreaded. She'd hoped that Uncle Pepper's was big enough that she'd be overlooked. The makeup Louise had suggested for the dim lighting was so different from what she normally wore that she thought it would be a disguise of sorts.

But staring into Rye's angry gaze convinced her she'd had no hope of disguise. The strange pull between them was too strong. She didn't understand the emotional attachment between them; she had no explanation for the intensity of it. But it was there, as real and as strong as the grip he had on her wrist. For the first time all evening, she was grateful that the band was loud.

"What can I get you?" she asked him, glad that the tremor in her voice couldn't be heard in the noisy nightclub. Rye's frown deepened.

"What are you doing here?"

Her chin went up a fraction. "I'm working. What can I get you to drink?"

"You can bring all of us a pack of Red Dogs, Lilly,"

Will called from the other side of the table, fairly shouting to be heard above the band.

Relieved to break contact with the searing blue of Rye's gaze, Lillian turned her head and made herself smile at the cowboy. "Right away."

She made a subtle scan of the number of men at the table, then started to pull away from Rye. She stiffened when he didn't let go. Heat blazed into her cheeks and she forced a small smile for the benefit of the men at the table who suddenly seemed spellbound by the silent interplay between her and Rye.

"Please, I need to get this order."

As if he were reluctant to let her go, he slowly released her wrist. The instant he did, she rushed away to get their drinks. When she returned with the beers, he watched grimly as she sat a bottle before each of them. Will paid for the drinks with a large bill, then magnanimously told her to keep the change. Lillian thanked him and hurried off, grateful to escape.

After that, she noted, Rye's expression was like granite. Because he was in a booth at the edge of her area, he could easily see every table she was responsible for. The fact that she often caught him staring at her left her more rattled and self-conscious than ever.

Lillian was grateful when he left the nightclub. Soon after, the band quit playing for the night, and Roy announced the last call for drinks. By the time the last customer was out the door, Lillian was so exhausted she could barely see straight.

Her feet were achy and swollen. Her brain was dazed and her eyes smarted from cigarette smoke. Her clothes reeked of smoke, food and beer, and she couldn't wait to get into a shower.

Fortunately, after Louise had hired her, she'd had the

presence of mind to ask if she knew of any rooms or apartments for rent. Louise had shown her the furnished apartment above the old part of the nightclub. Because Louise had been willing to wave a deposit and allow her to pay only two weeks' rent in advance instead of a full month, Lillian had snapped it up.

The inexpensive furniture and appliances had been in good shape and the apartment itself was clean. The small clothes washer and dryer unit in a closet were in working order. Eager to move in, she'd made two trips to lug her things from the motel that morning, then bought a set of sheets and towels, a blanket, a pillow and laundry soap from the Wal-Mart across the highway.

Now the thought of the freshly laundered sheets on the bed upstairs made her hurry to exit the nightclub and walk to the enclosed stairway that led to the second story. The parking lot was well-lit and customers were still leaving, so she had no fears of being bothered despite the late hour.

She got only a few feet from the nightclub door when she caught sight of a pickup parked near the base of the stairs. A tall cowboy leaned against the front fender, his arms crossed over his broad chest. His Stetson shaded his face from the security lights, but when he straightened and stepped onto the sidewalk, she knew it was Rye.

Lillian tensed. She was too powerfully drawn to him not to feel excited that he'd sought her out, but she was too ashamed of her predicament to welcome his attention now. Besides, he'd seemed angry in the nightclub. What could he possibly want? Because he was blocking her way, she stopped when she reached him.

"There's a diner up on the interstate," he said gruffly. "They serve breakfast any hour."

If it was an invitation, it was as ungracious as any she'd ever heard. She suddenly couldn't look at him. Her sense that he was trying to apologize in some roundabout way, to smooth things over, had to be the result of fatigue and loneliness and pain.

Her terse, "Sorry," and her move to step around him made him gently catch her arm as she passed. Lillian stopped abruptly, though he exerted no real restraint. She could feel his gaze on her profile.

"Something's real wrong, isn't it?"

The low question made the breath she was holding come whooshing out on a burst of emotion. If he'd said something nasty, if he'd been a jerk, she could have handled it. But it was the feel of his gentle grip on her arm and the clear concern in his low, rough voice that shook her reserve and threatened the severe control she had over her emotions.

It was several moments before she regained her composure enough to speak. "The other night you said you would forget me in a week," she said, unable to keep her voice from going higher and shakier with each word. "I wish you would."

His fingers moved on her arm and tightened, sending a shower of wonderful sensations through her that she tried to ignore. It was impossible. "We need to talk. Let me take you to breakfast."

"Maybe I'm not hungry," she said with soft defiance. "And I'm tired. My clothes smell, I smell—"

"Then take a quick shower and change your clothes. I'll wait."

He turned so they were facing the same direction. She could feel the heat of his body. "Come on, Lilly."

Lillian started to refuse, but he leaned so close that his warm breath gusted softly on her cheek. The tingles that cascaded over her skin sent a delicious weakness through her veins.

"Please."

While she could still think straight, she tilted her cheek away from his lips. His gruff, *Please,* was persuasive. She sensed the word was only a rare part of his vocabulary. "Why?"

"I'd like to talk."

"I'm not certain we have anything to say to each other," she asserted quietly.

"We could still have an early breakfast," he countered. "Where to? Same motel?"

Lillian shook her head, a bit leery of revealing where she lived to anyone. "Upstairs. I rented the apartment up there."

She felt his reaction to that, felt him stiffen and go still. She couldn't help but sense his disapproval.

"And you don't approve of that, either," she said softly. She pulled away from him and turned. "I think we should forget breakfast. Goodbye."

She started off, but he caught her arm again. "I'm sorry."

The sincerity in his low rough drawl brought her attention back to his face. She tried to search his eyes in the shadows beneath his hat brim. Because she didn't want to appear to give in to him as easily as she was, she said, "You don't say that often, do you?"

"No, I don't."

The candid admission hung between them. Lillian could see the sober cast of his stern features, could see the directness of his gaze. He was a hard man and a proud one. He was also rigid in his thinking. As she was. Before yesterday, she'd had her own opinions of nightclubs and the kind of women who worked in them.

Even now, if she'd felt she had any real choice, she wouldn't be working in a bar or living in an apartment over one. Should she fault him for thinking the same way?

"I'm tired. If a shower doesn't revive me, you'll have to leave and go to breakfast alone." She watched as the hard line of his mouth relaxed and curved faintly. She quickly added, "I could change my mind for other reasons, too."

"You could."

They stood there an uncomfortable moment before she turned and led the way to the enclosed staircase. Rye followed her, then reached past her to open the door once she'd unlocked it. Lillian preceded him up the dimly lit stairs, then unlocked the apartment door.

Once inside, she turned on a lamp in the small living room. She set her handbag on the dinette table in the kitchen. "Would you like some soda?"

At his, "Sounds good," she washed her hands, then got out the liter of soda she'd bought and an ice cube tray. In moments, she'd put ice in a disposable paper cup and added enough soda to fill it.

She left him and walked into the bedroom, closed the door, then went into the bath. She removed her makeup and jewelry, then stripped off her clothes and stepped into the shower. The water was hot and soothing, but after she got out and toweled off, she felt so sleepy she could barely keep her eyes open. When she went into the bedroom to sit on the side of the bed to dry her hair, it was even worse. The heat banished her tension and the whine of the motor lulled her.

By the time her hair was dry, she was sitting on the edge of the bed in a stupor. The week had been traumatic and stressful, her new job even more so. Unaccustomed to the noise, the frustration and being on her feet for hours the past two nights, she hurt all over, her craving for sleep so strong that she wasn't quite rational. A dreamlike fog descended and she realized that she would feel much better if she could just put her head down, just stretch out on the soft blanket and let her aching body relax a few moments...

Rye heard the hair dryer go off. He also heard the complete silence in the bedroom for several seconds before the central air conditioner cycled and the fan turned on. He waited ten minutes, then got up from the kitchen chair and walked to the bedroom door.

When he heard no sound on the other side, he quietly knocked. His firm, "Lillian?" got no answer, so he opened the door.

Lillian was stretched across the bed on her side. She was sleeping so hard that she didn't stir when he stepped in and walked over to the bed. He picked up her hair dryer and unplugged it before he set it out of the way on the night table.

He leaned down and tried to shake her gently awake. When she stirred, but stayed deeply asleep, he carefully gathered her into his arms. Because she was lying across the bed, he picked her up, then snagged the thick blanket and top sheet at the head of her bed and dragged them down.

He laid her gently in the middle of the bed. One of the hardest things he'd ever done in his life was to straighten her robe and leave it on her. Particularly when he realized she was naked underneath. By the time she woke up, the robe would be untied and open, and she'd probably be half out of it anyway, but he didn't let himself use that as an excuse. When he took Lillian Renard's clothes off, she'd damn well be awake for it.

As he pulled the covers over her, then adjusted the pillow beneath her head, he stared at her face. Her skin was perfect, smooth and unblemished. Her brows and lashes were as golden as her hair. The faint blush on her fair skin was the healthy kind and her lips were pink and lush. He hated the strong makeup she'd been wearing even more now that he could see close up just how naturally beautiful she was.

The rush of protectiveness that swept him made him feel so tender toward her that he hurt.

"What's wrong, Lilly?" he whispered, then tested the silkiness of her cheek with the back of a finger. Unable to resist, he braced a hand next to her pillow, then leaned down. He pressed his lips to her brow, then drew back and pressed a second kiss to the relaxed line of her mouth.

He was the only one who heard his gruff, "Good night, princess," before he switched off the light and walked out of the bedroom. He put the liter of soda and the ice cube tray away, privately appalled at the fact that the bottle of soda and the ice cubes were the entire contents of the refrigerator.

Though he wasn't one to snoop, he checked the cupboards. When every last one turned up empty, he had an explanation for the bag of paper cups on the counter. Feeling grim, he checked the lock on the apartment, then let himself out.

Tomorrow he'd find out why a woman like Lillian Renard was serving drinks and living in a cheap little apartment over a bar. If it had anything to do with any shenanigan of Rocky's, he and his brother were going to have a serious talk.

CHAPTER NINE

LATE the next morning, Rye rode in from a trip to the west range. By the time he'd got to bed in the wee hours that morning, he'd been tired enough to sleep like the dead. He lived by the rule "Early to bed and early to rise," but he'd suffered no ill effects from having a short night.

Though it was Sunday, he'd got up on time and was trying to get as much work done as possible before noon. He meant to be at Lillian's apartment by one o'clock. Dovey was already working on the cold lunch he would take with him. After he and Lillian shared the meal, he'd find out what the hell was going on.

He'd just dismounted at the stable and was about to lead his horse inside to unsaddle it when Joey's excited voice got his immediate attention.

"Rye! Come quick!"

Joey raced down the lane to the stable, not slowing until he was a few feet away. As if he'd just remembered he shouldn't spook the horse, he slid to a stop, then came forward at a brisk walk.

"Dovey says to come to the house quick. A real big truck is sittin' out front. From New York. He wants to know what to do with it." Joey had stopped and was fairly dancing with excitement.

"From New York?" Rye frowned at that. He called a stable hand from mucking out a stall and handed over his sorrel before he started for the house. Joey skipped along at his side and he reached out to affectionately ruffle the boy's hair.

"How do you know it's from New York, squirt?"

As if he were pleased to be able to provide the information, Joey burst out, "The driver said. And he said what's in the truck is for Miss Lillian. Whatdaya 'spose it is, Rye?"

A strange feeling tightened his chest. "We'll have to see," he said gruffly, then lengthened his stride.

Rye went around the house through the side yard. Joey gave up trying to hold back and raced ahead. The moment Rye saw that the "real big" truck was a large straight truck, he swore softly. The driver who was standing in the shade of the cab started toward him. They met at the edge of the front yard.

"I've got a delivery for Miss Lillian Renard," the driver told him.

"She's not here right now," Rye said smoothly. "What's it a shipment of?"

The driver consulted his clipboard. "Says here it's the complete inventory of her personal belongings, except for valuable jewelry. I guess that's coming by a courier service."

Rye nodded as if it were expected. "The trailer's completely full?"

The driver answered, "Yes, sir, it is. Almost all of it is boxed. There are a few large items—paintings and such—that were packed for the trip, but the trailer is full top to bottom, side to side, front to back."

"Why don't you and your partner come into the house?" Rye said with a tight smile as he started to move in that direction. "My cook can fix you a sandwich and a cold drink while I find out where you can unload everything."

"Great," the driver responded and motioned toward his partner in the truck cab. "We'd appreciate it. Been a long trip."

Rye led the way with Joey at his side. Once they were inside the house, he sent Joey ahead to Dovey and pointed the movers in the direction of the kitchen. He detoured to the dining room then out through the French doors to where Rocky was sunning herself on a chaise longue.

That she was lying in nothing but her sunglasses and the bottom half of a thong bikini infuriated him. He felt only disgust as he glared down at her, her breasts bared to the late morning sun. He picked up the beach towel she'd slung over a nearby chair and tossed it over her chest.

"For God's sake, cover up," he growled. "There's a seven-year-old boy around."

Rocky smiled up at him and pulled the towel aside to bare her breasts again. "There's also a big, tough uptight Texan around," she purred lazily.

He ignored her flirtation. "There's a truck from New York out front. The driver says it's full of Lillian's personal belongings."

Rocky continued to smile up coquettishly at him. "It probably is. Eugenia threatened to disown me if I marry Chad. So," she said, then giggled a bit, "she disowned little Goody Two-shoes to scare me. If that truck really is full of Lillian's things, then it's a new high in Grandmama's flair for the dramatic." Her smile faded to a smirk. "Where is my tiresome *half*-sister anyway? If she's still at that little motel, send the truck there. I'll get dressed and drive in so I'll be able to give Eugenia all the fun details."

A movement to the left drew Rye's attention briefly.

The sight of his brother didn't startle him, he was too angry. The brothers' eyes met somberly. Rye's voice was low. "Is this the woman of your dreams, little brother?"

Chad's tanned face flushed and his jaw tightened. "Thought so once." He glanced down at Rachel, just as unmoved by her nudity as his older brother. "Hope can make a man stupid." He met Rye's gaze levelly. "She'll be outta here today. You'd better see about that truck."

Rye nodded. He turned and stalked to the sliding patio door to the kitchen, relieved to see that the kitchen blinds had already been lowered to block the view. That meant no one in the kitchen could have seen their sunbathing guest.

He slid the big door open and moved the blinds aside only far enough to get in. Then he had a quick word with the movers and Dovey before he went to his room to shower.

Lillian began to awaken at noon. She rolled over to escape the sunlit brightness of the bedroom window, then winced when she rolled onto the loose knot of her robe belt. Still groggy, she tugged it out of the way. The nagging sense that something was wrong brought her closer to wakefulness.

Scenes of the night before went through her mind. The memory of Rye coming up to her apartment to wait while she showered and changed jolted her. She sat up suddenly and looked down at the robe she'd put on after her shower. The bedroom door stood open. Still not fully awake, she got up and rushed into the living room.

"Rye?" The word echoed dully in the stillness.

Had she fallen asleep? She hurried into the kitchen, dismayed when it, too, was empty. A quick check of the locked door, then of the empty parking lot below the front windows where his truck had been parked gave her an eerie sense of abandonment.

Eager to banish the uncomfortable feeling, she went back to the bedroom to dress and get ready for the day. Since Uncle Pepper's wasn't open on Sundays, the long day before her suddenly seemed bleak.

Rye pulled his pickup into the parking space near the bottom of the enclosed stairway and switched off the engine. He got out of the cab, then leaned across the seat for the picnic basket Dovey had packed. After he shut the door, he reached into the back of the truck for the cooler filled with soft drinks.

He carried the basket and the cooler to the stairway door, then pressed the buzzer. In a moment, he heard Lillian answer.

"Yes?"

"It's Rye. I've brought lunch."

He waited until he heard the buzz that released the door lock, then opened the door and stepped inside to begin the climb to Lillian's apartment.

Lillian opened the apartment door and leaned out to watch Rye ascend the stairs. The cooler and wicker basket he carried looked as if they were heavy. She stepped back and held the door for him.

"I hope you haven't eaten lunch yet," he said as he carried the basket past her to the table, then sat the cooler on the floor. "Dovey made us a cold lunch."

"Why would he do that?" Lillian watched him closely as he whipped off his hat and ran his strong fingers through his dark hair.

"Because he's a helluva cook and I told him to." He

upended the Stetson on a nearby counter and opened the basket.

Lillian watched, bemused as he set out packages of paper plates, plastic silverware and brightly colored plastic soft drink cups. The plastic containers of food he set out next provided a veritable smorgasbord of hot weather treats that included three kinds of salad, raw vegetables and dip, a selection of cold meats, condiments and a thick loaf of sliced bread. There was even a big bowl of chocolate pudding for dessert.

When he finished and lifted the cooler to a chair to open the top, she saw that a number of fruit juices and soft drinks had been pressed into the ice.

"My goodness, a feast," she said, then glanced up at him and smiled cautiously.

"Unless you'd rather see what the diner up on the interstate has to offer," he reminded her.

Lillian shook her head. "Are you joking? I really don't care to eat out—especially when there are cooks in the world like Dovey."

"Can you cook?"

The low question reminded her that he had no fondness for her "kind." She assumed he meant rich women who were too pampered to know how to do anything. In her case, he was right.

She shook her head, regretting to acknowledge another of the myriad of things she didn't know how to do. "We've always had cooks. I do know how to bake a few things, but I doubt anyone could live long on baked goods."

"So what will you do now?"

The question landed heavily. Lillian tried to conceal the surprise she felt. On the other hand, he had to have figured out by now that she'd lost her fortune.

Her voice was a bit hoarse as she replied with forced lightness, "I guess I'll learn to cook."

Rye smiled over at her, then reached for the package of paper plates. "I'll set the table if you'll open everything."

Lillian obliged, removing lids and arranging the food between them on the small table. Once she set out the condiments, Rye stepped over and pulled out her chair.

Lillian sat down and let him ease her closer to the table. She looked on as he motioned toward the cooler. He pulled her soft drink choice out of the ice, opened it then poured it into her plastic glass.

Lillian stared, not quite trusting this side of Rye. He sat down across from her, noticed she was looking at him, and went still.

Her soft, "Why?" was barely audible.

"Why what?" he asked mildly.

Lillian gave her head a small shake. "You're being so...pleasant."

Rye's face turned hard and his eyes glittered as he looked over at her. Lillian's heart sank.

"We got off on the wrong foot with each other," he said at last. "That was my fault."

The admission surprised her and she shook her head. The question, "What was wrong?" slipped out.

His expression turned harder. "At first, you reminded me of someone from a long time ago. Someone I despise. I realize now I was mistaken. You aren't at all like that person. The why of all this," he said, making a gesture to indicate the meal he'd brought, "is that I'd like to make it up to you. I'd like you to know I'm not a total s.o.b."

His blue eyes burned with an intensity she now recognized was a vital part of his personality. For some reason, he'd opened himself to her. The knowledge frightened as much as it delighted. A man like Rye Parrish would expect a reciprocal opening.

"Was she…" Lillian wasn't certain she should ask him for details. On the other hand, she'd experienced the harshness that had resulted from his contact with the person in his past whom he despised. She assumed it was a woman.

"It was a she," he confirmed gruffly. "And she was my mother."

Lillian's lips parted in surprise. He went on in the low, rough voice that she suddenly realized was evidence of strong or painful emotion.

"She was a Dallas socialite. Rich, spoiled and beautiful. My father made a fool of himself over her. She swore after I was born that she wanted no more children, and refused to have sex with him. Years later, when my father threatened to limit her to a monthly allowance because she was spending him into the poorhouse, she seduced him into changing his mind. He gave in, but her scheme backfired when she found out she was pregnant with Chad. She tried to have an abortion, but my father found out and paid her to go through with the pregnancy."

As if putting that much into words got him started, the rest of his story tumbled out in a blunt, shocking chronicle.

"I can't remember a single gentle touch from her, a single kind word. I learned cusswords at my mama's knee because she cussed me. I was always too dirty from play to touch, too 'wretched' when I was sick for her to nurse, and too noisy for her to allow in the house during the day.

"One day I caught her repeatedly slapping Chad—

who was a year old at the time—for spilling his orange juice. My father saw it, too, but he was so besotted, he did nothing but hire the foreman's wife to take care of us at her house during the day until he could be in the house at night to take care of us himself.

"She left us permanently before Chad turned two. She divorced our father and almost finished him off financially. Afterward, he worked himself into an early grave building everything back up, but he never stopped loving her, never stopped wishing she'd come back."

The silence fell like a thunderclap. Lillian stared over at him, appalled by the story, stunned that he'd told her so much, but sensing suddenly the kinship between them. She ached for the child he had been—cursed at, rejected and abused—ultimately abandoned by the woman who should have nurtured and loved him and his brother lavishly and unconditionally.

Her choked, "I'm sorry," was heartfelt and she reached across the table to place her hand on top of his.

Rye's gaze was so intense now that he was glaring over at her. She sensed the fierceness in him, the wounded child who'd been at the mercy of a heartless mother and a selfish father. When he turned his hand over and gripped hers, she felt the pain in him, the anger. What she'd sensed early on—that there was something hard and cruel and unforgiving in Rye Parrish—suddenly had an explanation. That those dark emotions were no longer aimed toward her was a relief.

"We'd better eat," he growled. "I didn't come here to talk about that."

Lillian shook her head. "I'm glad you told me. Thank you."

His fingers tightened gently on her hand before he released her. They filled their plates and ate in silence those first several minutes. Eventually, they both relaxed and Lillian asked about Joey and Buster.

"Buster's sore and pretty hobbled up by the cast on his front leg. Joey made him a bed in the corner of the kitchen so he can be near more activity, but not be out where he can get into trouble. Otherwise, the worst problem we have is that every time we let him outdoors, he makes a beeline for the swimming pool. He already got one cast wet last week that had to be replaced."

Lillian smiled at the story, then wiped her mouth on her napkin and leaned back to sip her soft drink. Rye was studying her face. The grimness she'd seen in him before descended. She sensed something was coming and tensed.

"Lillian, I've got some news that'll probably upset you," he said gently. "I'm sure it has to do with why you're living here and working down in the bar."

It was another hint that he'd guessed everything. She tried to maintain eye contact with the probing blue of his gaze, but she lasted only a couple moments. She stared down at her glass and slowly began to turn it on the tabletop.

"I've been..." Her voice trailed off breathlessly. She forced a smile, unaware that it was more grimace than smile. Her recent aversion to the word "disowned" made her pause and change what she'd been about to say. "I've done well this week," she said with false bravado. "I've found a job. Perhaps not one that fulfills a lifelong desire, but it's honest work all the same. I've found a place to live that I can afford..."

She made herself look over at him and struggled with her emotions. She was terrified she'd lose the fragile control she had over her pain and fear. She was terrified she'd cry.

She knew from experience that tears made her less attractive to family and friends. No one had ever cared enough about her to put up with her pain, not even her much adored father, who'd passed her to her nanny the moment everything wasn't sweetness and light. It was a sad fact of life that if she hadn't been perfectly behaved no one would have put up with her at all. She'd learned early to keep her hurts and disappointments to herself.

Besides, now that there was a precious bit of peace and understanding between her and this tough, macho Texan whom she was so strongly attracted to, she couldn't bring herself to risk doing something that was sure to ruin it all. She couldn't bear to break down and watch Rye's interest in her vanish.

His gaze was so direct it hurt her eyes. "Rachel says your grandma disowned you. If that's true, then I know about it, Lillian."

The admission almost broke her. A chill passed through her heart and the shaking started deep down. She tried to speak but it was hard to keep her words even. "You must understand...I can't talk about it. Not now." She stopped and couldn't help the little sniff that escaped her control. "Someday when it doesn't...bother me."

She was staring at him, making herself smile to give the impression that she wasn't really so upset. She was staring hard, doing her best to keep the tension in her body tight until this wave of emotion ebbed away...staring at his stern, handsome face, and watching it blur...

She suddenly sprang to her feet and began to match plastic lids to food containers. Frantic to work her way past the deluge that threatened, she tried to organize everything to put back in the wicker basket. She saw the slow movement across the table and knew that Rye had risen to his feet. He leaned forward and his big hands closed over hers.

"I'm sorry."

Lillian glanced up and gave him a smile. "Don't be. It's not your fault. You said you had some news. What is it?"

Rye watched her closely. "It'll keep."

She shook her head. "I'd rather know now." She suddenly couldn't look at him. His hands tightened consolingly on hers.

"Your grandma sent your things from New York." The terse statement told her all she needed to know. Though it had slipped her mind, she now recalled Eugenia telling her she'd be sending her things.

"Where are they?" she whispered.

"At the ranch. It'll all be safe there until you have time to deal with it. It's not in the way, so there's no hurry."

The first of the tears fairly spurted from her eyes. She pulled her hands from his and snatched a wad of paper napkins to press to her mouth. Her choked, "Excuse me," and her brisk rush to the bedroom almost wasn't fast enough.

She shoved the door closed, then hurried into the bathroom and closed the door firmly. She had the presence of mind to twist on the sink faucets to create a sound to cover her tears. A sharp knock on the bathroom door made her heart jump.

"Lillian?"

Her hasty, "I'm all right. Please—give me a few minutes," must have sent him away because he didn't knock again. Her fragile control crumpled.

Sobs tore at her chest, huge, gasping sobs that had her

reaching for a fresh bath towel to press over her face to stifle them. The sense of betrayal was acute. She couldn't remember a time when she hadn't worked for Eugenia's love. She'd fought hard not to be jealous of Rachel. Rachel who'd gone out of her way to be every bit the out-of-control, spoiled brat that their grandmother's steady overindulgence had produced. Rachel, who behaved outrageously, yet in Eugenia's sight, could do no wrong.

Lillian had been cast away to teach Rachel a lesson? She didn't think even Eugenia believed that. Lillian had been disowned because Eugenia had tired of her, because Eugenia had never warmed to the bastard grandchild she'd been forced to accept.

The opportunity to send Lillian to Texas before she withdrew her financial support had evidently been too attractive a vengeance for Eugenia to pass up. How better to vent her anger on the granddaughter she scorned than to send her to a rural area where she knew no one and where there were such limited means of financial survival?

The stark truth was bitter. Why should she cry over being disowned by such a witch? Lillian finally stopped and lowered the towel. She lifted her tear-ravaged face and stared into the mirror.

Eugenia Renard wasn't worth this grief. The sudden realization that she'd been freed from the impossible struggle for her grandmother's love and approval startled her. What Eugenia had meant to hurt her was actually for the best. Times might be difficult for her now, but she had a job, a place to live, and possibly a friend in Rye. She could make even more friends—friends who met her standards instead of Eugenia's. In two more years, she'd have access to her trust fund and she'd never have to worry about money again.

In the meantime, she'd no longer have to be that pathetically compliant little ninny who'd labored in vain all these years for a crumb of affection or approval from Eugenia Renard. She'd never again have to put up with being treated as poor relation or suffer being the hapless target of her grandmother's ire. For the first time since the traumatic phone call that had informed her she was disowned, Lillian realized she'd been handed more freedom than she'd ever imagined existed.

The notion thrilled her and she felt a sudden lightness of heart, a peace that began to ease through her and soothe some of the hurt. Until that moment, she hadn't fully realized how oppressive her life with Eugenia had been.

Now that Eugenia had banished her, the world was suddenly a brighter place, she was suddenly a happier person.

Not knowing quite what to think about these new feelings and impressions, and too cautious by nature to give them free rein, Lillian reached down and adjusted the water taps. She bent and washed her face, then took a few moments to pat cool water on her eyelids before she dried off and shakily set about reapplying her makeup.

Was Rye still out there? Her emotions were still raw enough that she didn't think she could bear it if he'd tired of waiting for her and had gone home. She hadn't meant to take so long. Though she now felt worlds better and actually felt an uncanny optimism about herself and her life, she'd left him for an unmannerly length of time.

Once she was certain she was presentable again, she was about to turn and leave the bathroom when another knock sounded on the bathroom door.

"Lillian? Are you all right?"

The low, rough sound of Rye's voice brought a fresh wave of emotion. Did he care about her?

"Lilly?" The concern in his voice made her eyes sting.

"I'm all right," she got out, but hesitated to open the door.

"Is there anything I can do?"

The question flooded her with tenderness toward him. Her sudden instinct—that Rye Parrish had the potential be a true and loyal friend—gave her the most profound feeling of warmth and safety she'd ever felt in her life.

She forced a soft smile and quietly opened the door. Rye had braced a hand against the door frame and was looking down at her.

"Feel better?"

Her quick, "Yes," was a bit breathless.

"You look better," he remarked, then reached over with his free hand to catch a strand of her light hair and smooth it back into place. His sharp gaze studied her face for a long moment, and she felt as if he could see everything. "Calmer."

"I'm sorry I took so long. I didn't mean to—"

Rye touched a gentle finger to her lips. "No need to be sorry. I just…worried. It's a helpless feeling when you want to comfort someone and they won't let you."

Lillian stared up at him, emotional again. "It's a big risk, you know. Most people pretend to care, but they really don't. God help you if you ever put them to the test."

Rye shook his head. "Most *bastards* pretend to care," he corrected grimly. "Most of the others care, but they don't know what to do about it." He straightened and softened his tone. "Sounds to me like you've been hangin' around the wrong kinda people, Lilly. Maybe we can do better for you out here now.''

Lillian glanced down to escape the wonderful intensity in his eyes. The insecurities of a lifetime burst up. ''Do you think I can ever fit in here?''

''You can do anything you want to, Lillian.'' He held his hand out to her.

Lillian hesitantly slipped her hand into his.

''Why don't we go out to the ranch?'' he said as his thumb rubbed gently over the back of her hand. ''You can swim if you want, we can have supper. After it cools off, we can go riding. Watch the sunset and wait for the stars to come out.''

She thought instantly of Rachel and how much the glad prospect of going to the ranch dulled because of her spiteful presence. ''What about Rachel?''

Rye's expression went stern. ''Last I heard, she was leaving the ranch today.''

''Is the engagement off?''

''It is as far as Chad's concerned,'' he said, then asked, ''Do you think it'll make a difference in your situation?''

Lillian shook her head and glanced away. ''I think this was an opportunity Eugenia was waiting for. Even if she changes her mind about disowning me, I won't go back to living with her. Not after this.''

Before he got the idea she was still heartbroken about it all, she looked up at him and said, ''What's that saying I keep hearing? 'Been there, done that'?'' Her smile was still a bit forced, but then, she might always carry a sadness about it all.

Rye leaned down and kissed her softly. She was struck by the sweetness of it, and though he didn't touch her in any other way, she reached up hesitantly and placed her palm gently on his strong jaw.

They ended the kiss at the same time. Lillian stood there a moment, her eyes shut, savoring the sweet feeling that lingered. She opened her eyes, then glanced away, suddenly self-conscious.

That was the moment she realized she was falling in love with Rye Parrish.

CHAPTER TEN

WHEN they walked in the front door at the ranch later that afternoon, Joey's high young voice called out, "Hey, Dovey! It's Miz Lilly!"

The boy's excitement made Lillian feel welcome. Before Rye got the door closed, Joey ran to her, then skidded to a halt and fidgeted uncertainly. When Lillian smiled and leaned down, he threw himself at her and gave her a brief hug around the neck before he sprang back, as if such a display of affection was somehow not manly.

"Did ya come to see your stuff, Miz Lilly?" he asked eagerly.

She felt Rye stiffen beside her and she smiled at the boy. "I also came to visit. How's Buster doing?"

With that, Joey led the way to the kitchen, but before they got there, Buster hobbled from his corner to greet them at the door and give a hoarse woo-woo-woof!

"Here she is, Buster," Joey told his dog, then grabbed the big animal around the neck. "I tol' ya Rye'd bring her back." Buster kept coming forward as if Joey's slight weight was no deterrent. "Uh-oh, Rye, he ain't gonna stop!"

Buster found a burst of speed and hurtled awkwardly at Lillian, then tried to jump up. Because one of his front legs had a cast all the way to his shoulder, and most of his body was wrapped snugly in what resembled ace bandages, Buster was even more heavy and clumsy and huge than before. Nevertheless, he managed to jump up on Lillian and make her stagger to keep her balance.

Rye rescued her, catching the dog around the chest, taking care with the unwieldy cast as he carefully lowered the big dog to his feet. Buster yelped softly, but it was hard to tell whether it was from excitement or the strain on his battered body. His big tongue slurped wildly at the three of them.

"Come on, dog," Rye scolded gently as he carefully eased the dog into a turn. He managed to alternately walk and scoot the animal back to his pallet with Joey alongside to help.

Buster craned his neck to look back pleadingly at Lillian. A bubble of compassion and laughter tumbled out of her as she watched the dog's comically woebegone face. Feeling sorry for the injured animal, she hurried over to the pallet, then got on her knees to help coax the big pup to lie quietly on his side.

Exhausted by the activity, the animal let his big head flop onto the pillow and laid still. Lillian rubbed him around the ears, then gently stroked his head. Buster heaved a huge sigh of contentment and closed his eyes, his tail thumping happily on the floor.

"I think that dog's smitten with Miz Lillian," Dovey commented as he looked on. "No doubt about it."

"What's smitten?" Joey piped up, then looked to Rye.

Lillian suddenly felt Rye's gaze on her and glanced over at him. As if he'd been waiting to have her attention, he answered, "If you're smitten with someone, it means you suddenly fall in love with them. It's not something you expected to happen, but when it does, you fall hard."

"So Buster's in love with Lilly?"

Rye broke eye contact with her to answer the boy. "In a dog's way of loving people, he probably does."

"Oh." Joey appeared to be thinking about it as he carefully patted his dog. "So maybe Lilly should stay so Buster will be happy."

The boy's remark startled Lillian. Rye's gruff, "Maybe so," warmed her, but she was suddenly too self-conscious to look at either of them.

Fortunately, Joey himself changed the subject, telling Rye he'd done his chores and asking if he and two other boys who lived on the ranch could go swimming. Lillian relaxed as she listened to Rye review the rules about using the pool.

Things had changed dramatically between her and Rye, but she wasn't certain what any of it meant. She declined an invitation to swim, but she and Rye sat in the shade on the patio drinking iced tea while they supervised Joey and his two friends as they frolicked in the water.

Rye was the perfect host. Later, he showed her the three unused guest rooms where he'd had her things stored, then reminded her again that everything could stay where it was, indefinitely if need be.

They learned from Dovey that Rachel had indeed packed and left the Parrish Ranch for good. They all assumed she'd caught the first plane going anywhere at the airport. Now that she was gone, Chad had retreated to one of the line cabins on the other end of the ranch. To think things over, Dovey said.

Supper was a pleasant chaos with Joey and the two boys. Afterward, Dovey took over the chore of supervising the boys while Rye and Lillian went for a long horseback ride. They watched the sunset from a creek bank, then walked their horses back to the stables at a slow enough pace that the stars came out long before they were in sight of the ranch headquarters.

The visit was wonderful for Lillian. The ability to relax and enjoy simple things was an unexpected pleasure. Life was so much slower here, and now that there was peace between her and Rye, she was much less tense and self-conscious than she could ever remember being.

Though it still hurt to be rejected by her family, Lillian was somehow comforted by being with Rye, watching the boys' antics and Buster's, and stuffing herself on Dovey's wonderful cooking.

She hated when it was time for Rye to drive her back to her apartment. Their long kiss goodnight was passionate, but ultimately left Lillian feeling more lonely than ever when Rye released her and started reluctantly down the stairs to go home.

Lillian realized as she watched him go that she wasn't just beginning to fall in love with the big Texan—she already had.

Lillian began to adapt to her new life. Weeknights at Uncle Pepper's were much less crowded and chaotic than the previous Friday and Saturday nights had been. The regular house band, Otis, was quite good, and Lillian found herself beginning to like the country-western music they played.

Because the pace was much less hectic, it was easier to handle the food and drink orders. She memorized the menus in no time, and began to relax with the customers. Though the patrons were mostly working class folk who held agricultural jobs in the area, Lillian warmed quickly to the natural friendliness of everyone.

She even made friends with the women she worked with. It thrilled her to be included in their gossip about the customers and their own families, husbands and boy-friends. For someone who'd had her friends selected for her her whole life, the sudden freedom to make new ones was exciting.

Meanwhile, she spent more and more time at the Parrish Ranch. The first week, Rye came to town on Sunday and Thursday, her days off, to take her to the ranch to visit and sort through her things. After that, she also got to spend a few afternoons during the week at the ranch before she went to work.

Hating that her belongings were taking up space in Rye's home, she brought several boxes back to her apartment each time she visited the ranch. The boxes mostly contained her clothes, boxed according to season. Everything that had been in her drawers and closets at any of Eugenia's residences had been sent along.

She sorted through her clothing, shoes and costume jewelry, then separated out the things she was no longer interested in wearing. She asked at work about a local charity to donate them to, but was instead invited to bring her things to add to a garage sale one of the women was having with her sister in another small town nearby.

The large garage sale turned out to be a wonderful social activity that Lillian enjoyed immensely with her new friends. To her delight, the inexpensive prices on her quality items made everything sell out by the end of the day, and she came home with a surprising amount of money.

In the meantime, the money Eugenia had promised arrived via Western Union. But now that Lillian was making her own money, she wired Eugenia's money back to her. Her better jewelry arrived by courier soon after.

Lillian was adapting well and making a life for herself. She was more happy than she'd ever been. And each hour she spent with Rye she fell even more deeply in love.

She'd worked at Uncle Pepper's for nearly four weeks when she got the early morning call from New York. Harriet Davies, her grandmother's personal secretary, was on the line.

"Lillian, dear, it's your grandmama. I'm afraid she's gravely ill."

The words jolted Lillian awake. "What's wrong?"

"Well, as you know her heart has been giving her trouble for years," Ms. Davies reminded her. "She's had an episode and she's asking for you. I've arranged for a private jet to pick you up at that little airport. It will fly you straight to New York. Allister will meet you with the car and bring you directly to her bedside."

Alarmed, Lillian sat up in her bed. If there was this much rush for her to return to New York, Eugenia had to be very ill indeed. "She's that ill then?" she asked softly, suddenly emotional.

"Madam is very ill. I advise haste, Lillian. Haste."

The grim words weighed heavily on her. In the light of her grandmother's grave condition and possibly her impending death, all Lillian's angry thoughts about her suddenly seemed mean and disloyal.

"Lillian?"

Lillian clutched the phone receiver and got out a hoarse, "I'm here."

"Your plane will arrive by one p.m., your time, at the same airport you arrived at. The pilot will have you paged in the terminal," she said, then went on in the brisk, efficient—bossy—manner she was known for. "Since it's just now seven a.m., six hours should allow you plenty of time to set your affairs in order, pack and travel to the airport.''

Lillian said quickly, "Yes. I'll be there.''

"Very well. You have the number here if there's a problem. Have a safe trip.''

The line went dead so abruptly that it had to be a record of sorts for the woman. Lillian reached to press the disconnect button, got a dial tone, then called Parrish Ranch.

It was a relief when Dovey answered and instantly handed the phone over to Rye. The moment she heard his low, "What's wrong, baby?'' she felt the tears start. Because he knew she worked late, he'd guessed right away that a seven a.m. call from her must mean something was wrong.

When she told him that her grandmother was gravely ill, his instant, "I'll be right there,'' was a comfort.

As she raced to get ready and pack her suitcases, she realized suddenly that she was afraid to leave Texas. At first, she thought it was because she dreaded the outcome of her grandmother's illness. But the moment Rye walked in, she knew it was because she didn't want to leave him.

The knowledge that she would miss Rye terribly made her even more emotional, though she tried to put on a brave face for him. He took her to breakfast at the diner on the interstate, then, since the ranch was on the way to the airport, they made a stop there.

Lillian hadn't wanted to suddenly leave without telling Joey where she was going and why she had to go.

"Can Rye and me come with you, Lilly?''

Joey's question broke her heart. She couldn't help hugging him tightly for several moments. "No, sweetheart, not this time. Hospitals aren't fun places to wait around in for busy boys like you," she said, then drew back a bit to stroke his cheek. "But I'll call you and Rye every day and I won't be gone one minute longer than I have to be."

"But we're going to see the judge so Rye can be my guardian. You'll miss that," he reminded her, and Lillian's heart twisted. "And my birthday party is after that."

Lillian hugged him tightly. "I know, sweet. We can hope I'll be back by then or that maybe I can get away. I'll try, but I can't make any promises now. I don't know how long my grandmama will be so sick."

Joey clung to her and pressed his hot little face into her neck. "I'm just gonna miss you, is all."

"And I'll miss you, too."

Lillian made a quick call to Louise to tell her the situation. Louise's quick, "Don't you worry, honey, just look after your grandma," was a huge relief. They started for the airport after an early, light lunch. Rye was grim, Joey was subdued and a bit whiny, and Lillian was torn. She didn't know how she'd come to love Rye and Joey so deeply and so completely. She hated to leave them, yet she hated to stay away from New York.

She was so troubled and guilty about the choice she'd made that she was almost sick by the time they reached the airport. It was Rye who finally set her mind at ease. He sent Joey to the little airport snack bar that was in sight of where they stood, then turned toward her and took her into his arms. The kiss he gave her was brief and sweet.

"Don't worry about anything," he said gruffly. "Joey and I don't want you to go, but we don't want you to stay here and feel bad, either. Your grandma is sick and she's asking for you. I understand why you have to go."

Lillian looked up at him with tear-blurred eyes. "Thank you for understanding."

Rye gave her a wry twist of lips. "I'm a real understanding hombre."

Lillian grinned through her tears and hugged him tightly. Too soon, she was paged and instructed where to go to meet her plane. The three of them carried her luggage to the aircraft and while the pilot loaded it, she tried to say goodbye.

She hugged and kissed little Joey, then let Rye take her in his arms for a last kiss. The three of them stood together on the tarmac, Rye holding little Joey on one arm while he held her against him with the other. Lillian hugged them both for as long as she could. Then, after a last sad kiss for each of them, she pulled away and fled to her plane.

The small private hospital featured tastefully decorated rooms with artwork on loan from an art museum.

Eugenia, the nurse told her, was resting comfortably in one of the elegant private rooms. Lillian was relieved to find out her grandmother wasn't in the intensive care unit, and she began to feel hopeful. She tapped softly on the closed door. Ms. Davies answered almost instantly.

"Lillian—you're here at last," Ms. Davies exclaimed in a stage whisper. "Just one moment. I'll see if she's ready to receive you."

The big door hissed shut. Lillian waited nervously. It took so long for Ms. Davies to return that she started to pace. She dreaded seeing Eugenia, as much because she was terrified to see her so ill as she was to have to come face-to-face with the grandmother who'd disowned her.

Ms. Davies returned at last and opened the door just wide enough to usher Lillian inside. Lillian immediately looked toward the hospital bed. A heart monitor beeped quietly next to the bed. Eugenia lay still, an IV attached to her left arm, the head of her bed inclined, but not in a fully upright position. Her grandmother's silver hair was carefully brushed and arranged, her stern face chalky except for a bit of lipstick and two bright spots of rouge on her cheeks. It was no surprise to Lillian that her grandmother would be wearing makeup. Eugenia was vain about her personal appearance.

At Ms. Davies's prompting, Lillian approached the bedside. She hesitantly put out her hand to touch the manicured and beringed fingers that lay limply on the coverlet.

Because Eugenia was by nature an unaffectionate woman who spurned emotional gestures, Lillian felt uncomfortable taking hold of her hand. She thought suddenly how wonderful and easy it was to touch little Joey, to smooth his hair back, to kiss his cheek, to give him a hug. How could Eugenia have resisted hugging and kissing her granddaughters when they were so little and so in need of motherly affection? How could Lillian express her affection and concern now for an old woman who'd scorned such gestures as foolish sentimentality?

"Lillian?" Eugenia's voice still carried the cultured tone it always had, but it was so weak, so whispery, that Lillian ignored her reservations and gently gripped her grandmother's hand.

"I'm here, Grandmama," she whispered, nearly overcome. "How are you?"

Eugenia's head moved on the pillow and she turned her face toward Lillian. "Lillian?"

"Yes, Grandmama."

The elderly woman opened her eyes. The sharp intelligence Lillian had seen in her grandmother's gaze all her life blazed up at her as keen as ever. But the impression vanished so suddenly that Lillian realized she must have imagined it.

Eugenia's eyelids instantly lowered to half-mast and trembled. Her blue eyes dulled and began to wander as if she barely had the strength to focus. "Lillian..."

She was alarmed when Eugenia's strength suddenly gave out. She gripped her grandmother's delicate hand and glanced anxiously at Ms. Davies, who now stood on the other side of the bed.

Ms. Davies shook her head sadly. "Just passed out again, poor dear. She's had almost no strength."

"What does the doctor say?" Lillian demanded softly.

"That perhaps with time and gentle care..." Ms. Davies's voice trailed away noncommittally. "He refuses to make predictions."

Lillian gave her an impatient look. "I want to speak to him. Right away."

Ms. Davies's brows went up and she gave a half nod, half shake of her head that seemed evasive to Lillian. "Perhaps tomorrow."

"Then I'll speak to someone at the nurse's station," Lillian insisted. Ms. Davies shook her head.

"They have strict orders not to discuss her case with anyone. You know ..ow the press would pry and how any leaks of information could be misconstrued and possibly damaging to Renard business interests. You must trust that your grandmama is in competent hands, Lillian, and that I am watching over her as I have always done."

Ms. Davies glanced down in obvious concern at Eugenia's pale face. "Allister can drive you home for the evening. There will be no need for you to wait here, since I will inform you of any change. You may return in the morning. Hopefully, your grandmama will be more rested by then and will perhaps be stronger.''

Lillian looked down anxiously at her grandmother. ''I'd like to stay.''

''Oh, Lillian, you know how Eugenia hates anyone to see her when she's not at her best,'' Ms. Davies reasoned. ''Please. Tomorrow will be a better time for you to be here, when she's awake and might know it. She will hate it if you hover throughout the night.''

Lillian knew Ms. Davies was right. She looked over at the older woman. ''You'll let me know the instant anything changes, for better or worse?'' she asked urgently.

Ms. Davies gave a curt nod. ''You have my word on that, dear.'' Her stern face softened into a rare smile. ''Go on now. Have Allister drive you home. Cook has prepared a supper that includes several of your favorite dishes.''

Lillian gave her grandmother's hand a gentle squeeze and said a soft, ''Goodnight, Grandmama. I love you,'' before she reluctantly placed the slim hand back on the coverlet. She wouldn't have dared to kiss her grandmother's cheek. She said a quick, ''Goodnight, Ms. Davies,'' and turned to leave.

''Lillian?'' Ms. Davies's call made her stop and glance back. ''Welcome home,'' she added, then gave another rare, but stiff smile.

''Thank you. Goodnight.''

''Goodnight to you, Lillian,'' Ms. Davies called quietly after her.

Lillian stepped outside the door and fought to keep the tears back. Worry made her steps leaden as she walked down the hall to the elevator, then went downstairs to find Allister. The limo ride to Eugenia's penthouse seemed to take forever and Lillian watched, disinterested, as the city sights raced past her window in a blur.

"You've missed your calling, Harriet. Your thespian abilities suddenly make me wonder how many performances you've treated me to over the years."

Eugenia Renard sat regally on her hospital bed, her blue satin bed jacket on and the silk bedspread folded across her lap with military precision. The screen of the heart monitor was dark, but the IV was still in place. She was peering at her face in a gilded hand mirror.

"It was not I who thought up this scheme," Harriet Davies retorted with a candor that bespoke their forty year association.

Eugenia's low, "Hmmm," as she lowered the mirror and glared at her assistant was a rebuke. "You don't approve, do you?"

"You know I don't. You sent that child out to the frontier, then financially cut her off. Now you're upset because you don't approve of the life she's making for herself or the man she's falling in love with. I'd say, you gave up the right to have a say in anything Lillian does or wants to have."

Eugenia's eyes narrowed on her assistant. "You've always favored Lillian."

Harriet Davies straightened her shoulders and lifted her chin. "It's hard not to favor a genuinely sweet, thoughtful person. Lillian is the granddaughter you should have treasured, Eugenia. Even though you disowned her, all it took was one call and she was on her way here with nothing on her mind but how ill you are."

Harriet took a deep breath and went on with daring sarcasm, "On the other hand, Rachel, your favorite, was generous enough to leave a California telephone number where someone who knows someone who *might* know her whereabouts could relay a message—just in case you take a turn for the worst.''

Eugenia's face flushed and she hissed out a low, ''Enough!''

''Yes, it is enough, Eugenia. I will only carry on with this charade for a brief time. This lie is so horrific that I may be imperiling my immortal soul, but I owe you a debt from long ago. In two weeks, I shall consider that debt paid in full. You shall then receive my official letter of resignation.''

''You'll never resign,'' Eugenia declared, then snickered.

Harriet calmly folded her hands at her waist and raised her graying brows.

''I'm sorry I didn't call sooner. It took me longer than I thought to get time to myself. Is Joey still awake?'' Lillian asked Rye late that evening.

''Still awake, waiting for your call,'' Rye told her, and Lillian felt a pang at the drawl in his low voice. Already she missed his lazy Texas accent. ''Here he is.''

''Lilly? Are you in New York now? Rye gave me this map to look at,'' Joey told her eagerly, then went on to describe the map of the United States that Rye had tacked up in his bedroom. ''We brought a phone into my bedroom tonight in case you called at my bedtime.''

Lillian smiled at the boy's chatter. When Joey had exhausted his run-through of what had happened at the ranch from the time she'd left until that very moment, he bid her a somber little goodbye that made her eyes sting.

Then Rye got on the line and asked about Eugenia.

"I should know more after I speak to the doctor tomorrow. Ms. Davies, her personal assistant, clearly didn't want to go into detail. Probably in case Grandmama prefers to inform me herself." Lillian hesitated, then went on in a lower voice. "If she's able to, that is. She was so weak this evening she could barely speak, Rye. But she opened her eyes and said my name, so I think she knows I'm here now."

The rest of their conversation was along the same vein. When Rye asked if Rachel was also there, Lillian realized no one had mentioned her sister.

"To tell the truth, I've scarcely given her a thought," Lillian confessed, feeling a bit guilty. "I'll ask, but she must not be here at the penthouse or she would have made her presence known by now."

Shortly after that, their conversation wound down and Lillian bid Rye a quiet goodbye. Afterward, she went straight to bed. She laid awake in the dark a long time, but her mind was more fixed on Rye and Joey and Texas than it was on her grandmother or her sister.

To Lillian's relief, Eugenia's condition began to turn around. Her first morning at the hospital found Eugenia awake and already sitting in a chair. Of course, Eugenia became weary almost immediately and Ms. Davies and the private nurse had to help her back into bed.

Unfortunately, the doctor had made his rounds before six a.m. that day, so Lillian missed her chance to speak to him. The private nurse did take her into the hall at one point to explain that Eugenia's sudden progress had surprised the doctor. She then suggested Lillian's arrival was the cause.

For someone who'd never felt loved by her grandmother, or even particularly wanted by her, the notion that Eugenia felt at least enough for her to be buoyed by her presence rekindled every childish hope she'd ever had about her grandmother loving her.

But that night, when she confessed as much to Rye, his grim, "Be careful, Lillian," hurt her feelings.

"You don't think it's possible her illness has changed her attitude toward me?" she ventured softly.

"I hope it has, baby, but I don't trust her," he said bluntly, then softened a bit. "I'm sorry."

The mere suggestion that Eugenia had an ulterior motive—that her improvement had nothing to do with Lillian's presence—was tantamount to telling Lillian she wasn't very lovable.

Her spirits dragged so low that not even his gruff, "I care about you and don't want you to be hurt," brought them completely back to the soaring heights they'd been at prior to her calling him.

The next two days, Eugenia's condition improved so remarkably that she was allowed to go home. Of course, Ms. Davies hired private nurses to be on hand around the clock, so Eugenia had nearly the level of care at home that she'd had in the hospital.

Meanwhile, after her first week and a half in New York, Lillian's daily phone calls to Rye began to deteriorate. He didn't seem to understand that she wanted to stay on a bit longer, even though the life-or-death crisis had long since passed. Eugenia actually became teary whenever the subject of Lillian returning to Texas came up, so Lillian wanted to make certain Eugenia was truly on the mend before she did anything that might upset her.

Near the end of the second week, Rye seemed faintly impatient with that. But then, because she'd stayed so long, she'd had to miss the court date. They were all disappointed about that, but things had gone well, and Rye was now Joey's legal guardian.

Lillian assured Rye that she was eager to return to Texas, and that she was already preparing Eugenia. Even if her grandmother was not well enough for Lillian to move back permanently yet, she could at least return in time for Joey's birthday party and stay a few days. Since the party was scheduled for a week from the following Sunday, and she'd already purchased her plane tickets and the gift, she had no worries about keeping her word to attend.

It shocked her a bit when Rye seemed not to believe her.

"Lilly," he said, his voice low and rough. "I reckon I know how much home means to a person, even if home is in New York."

He paused and Lillian felt her heart begin to race. "Rye—"

"No, baby, let me finish," he cut in. "Maybe you don't really know what you want. It could be this thing with your grandma took you back to New York so you can have a firsthand reminder of the life you were meant for. Before it's too late."

Her quick, "No—Rye—"

"I'm not blaming you, Lilly. Some things just aren't meant to be."

"Yes they are," she insisted as she gripped the receiver.

"Maybe you need to give it more thought," he said, then finished with sudden gruffness. "I need to get some sleep. We're shipping a bull early tomorrow. Goodnight, Lilly. Take care."

And then he was gone. The dial tone droned in her ear for several seconds before she recovered enough to hang up. He hadn't waited for her to respond. It seemed as if he'd felt compelled to say his piece then hang up before she could say anything to refute it.

Some things just aren't meant to be. The low words made her chest ache. The reminder that his mother and father's crazy union had tormented him, and that his mother's mistreatment and later abandonment had scarred him, suddenly gave clarity to what had just happened.

If Rye was worried she might be extending her visit because she favored the same lifestyle his mother had preferred, it was no wonder he was suspicious of her ongoing absence. If he believed history was repeating itself, he'd be just as hard to convince and just as driven to put an end to their relationship as he'd seemed to be tonight.

Lillian started to call him back, then paused and hung up the phone. She was giving a lot of weight to Rye's past, laying a lot of blame at his mother's door.

But what if she were mistaken? What if Rye had lost interest in her? Lillian leaned back in her chair as the insecurities of a lifetime stirred. Everything had happened so quickly between them.

What if her extended visit to New York had become a secret relief to him? If he'd come to realize that he didn't care that much for her, then his suggestion for her to give things more thought made sense.

Maybe you don't really know what you want, he'd said before he'd added the part about the life she was "meant" for.

If Rye's interest in her was waning, then his suggestion that she was delaying her return to Texas because she preferred her New York lifestyle, gave them both an easy way out of the relationship.

Lillian felt her spirits plummet.

CHAPTER ELEVEN

THE next day passed slowly. Lillian slipped into her room at ten p.m. to place her call to Texas.

"Miz Lillian, the boss and Joey went over to a barbecue at the Nelson's tonight," Dovey told her. "He said not to expect him home till late. Joey's stayin' all night with the kids, so he had no worries about the boy being up too late."

Lillian couldn't speak for a moment. Her, "Thank you, Dovey. I didn't know," was hoarse.

"Thought sure he'd mentioned it to you. How's your grandma?" he asked kindly.

"Improving each day, Dovey. How are things at the ranch?"

"Same as usual, only hotter and dustier this time of year. Hope to see you back here soon," he said, and Lillian smiled briefly.

"I hope to be back soon," she insisted. "I'll try calling tomorrow night, then. Tell Rye and Joey I'm sorry I missed them and I hope they had a good time."

"I'll give them the message, Miz Lillian. You take care now."

Her soft, "You, too, Dovey," was choked.

She hung up the phone as a feeling of dread wrapped around her heart.

Early the next afternoon, the phone at Parrish Ranch rang. Rye was working in the den, so he picked it up before the second ring.

"Mr. Parrish? This is Louise Pepper over at Uncle Pepper's. Somethin's goin' on over here with that apartment I rented to Lilly Renard, and I just want to make sure everything's on the up 'n' up. I tried to call her at the number she left me, but couldn't get no answer. I figure since you're a friend of hers, you'd know somethin'."

"What's wrong?"

"There was a movin' truck out here when Roy and I got to the bar a few minutes ago. They'd just about finished packin' up Lilly's things and loadin' 'em. When we asked what was goin' on, one of the men showed me his paperwork. He said Lil'd sent them to move her things and give back the key. Since she didn't call us herself, and we can't get through on the number she gave us, we thought we'd better ask you about it."

Rye felt the old anger stir and a bitter taste filled his mouth. "I don't know anything about it," he said grimly. "If everything looks official to you, then there's nothing can be done. If you think it looks suspicious, call the sheriff."

"Roy thinks I outta—" Louise cut herself off, then said, "Hold on a minute, Mr. Parrish."

Rye listened as Louise talked to Roy, who must have been standing close by. He heard her puzzled, "You don't say," then waited for her to return.

"Yeah, here's somethin'," she said, speaking to him again. "Roy was flippin' through the mail and found a letter from Lilly sayin' she's got to quit her job on account of her grandma's health. She's sent a check to cover her rent and utilities, and says she's sendin' movers to get her things and give me the key. I guess now it looks like Roy and me got excited over nothin'. Sorry to bother you."

Rye gave a rough-voiced, "No problem," and hung up the phone.

The red haze of anger that blazed up filled his mind. He reached for the phone, punched the number Lillian had given him, then slammed the receiver down when he got no answer.

The next three nights, Lillian's calls to the Parrish Ranch were picked up by an answering machine. Her brief messages, along the lines of a semi-cheery, "Sorry I missed you, hope all is well," hadn't inspired any call-backs.

By the next evening, she couldn't explain away her sense that something was wrong. Rye was either angry that she hadn't returned to Texas, or he'd lost interest in her.

She'd told him about buying a plane ticket that would get her to Texas in plenty of time for Joey's birthday party. He had to have already received the present she'd bought and sent by express mail to the ranch for safe-keeping. How could he not believe she meant to be there soon?

But maybe she'd got it all wrong. Maybe Rye had lost interest in her. Her return to New York and the spoiled jet-set life Rye imagined she had might have reminded him too much of his mother. And because there was probably nothing more detrimental to a man's feelings of romance or desire than for a woman to remind him of his mother, his feelings for her had changed.

What else could his sudden avoidance mean?

The hurt she felt squeezed the air from her lungs. She was in love with Rye and she'd thought he might be in love with her. She'd pictured returning to Texas, getting her job back and living at her little apartment while she and Rye spent more time together and explored how they felt about each other.

Though living in Texas had been forced upon her, she'd managed to make a good start at a life there. But if Rye didn't want her, she couldn't bear to imagine living in his orbit and being excluded from his life. And little Joey's. She'd gotten so attached to the child...

Eugenia's brisk, "Lillian, dear, please come in to see me," made her pull herself together and start reluctantly for the hall.

"Lillian, don't be tiresome. I'm getting stronger every day. I've been planning this party for weeks and I won't hear of canceling it."

"What does your doctor say?" Lillian asked.

"He says I may do anything I feel up to. I feel up to this and with you to share the duties of hostess with me, I don't foresee a problem." Eugenia paused and looked over at Ms. Davies. "And since Ms. Davies has so graciously consented to remain in my employ, everything will run faultlessly under her supervision. As usual."

Lillian smiled. There had been a minor crisis that week. Harriet Davies had handed Eugenia her resignation. It had taken most of that day for Eugenia to reason with her long-time assistant and work out the "new" agreement Harriet had insisted upon.

It rather surprised Lillian that Eugenia had given in. Eugenia never backed down, never made agreements with subordinates that required anything special of her. As a result, Lillian didn't believe for a moment that the squabble had been over a raise—as Eugenia had confided to her. Money might be part of it, but there was definitely something else at stake. Something Lillian sensed, but couldn't guess.

"I understand you didn't buy a new gown this afternoon," Eugenia went on. "Does this mean you'll be wearing the new ivory silk?"

Lillian shook her head. "The ivory silk is in Texas."

Eugenia quickly disagreed. "It's hanging in the winter closet, dear. If you won't be wearing it, you must start early tomorrow and find something else. This party is very important to me."

The sudden silence rolled over the three of them like a shock wave. Lillian was watching when the flash of surprise crossed Eugenia's face, followed instantly by an ill-humored scowl.

Ms. Davies raised a hand as if to get Eugenia's attention, but the minute Lillian glanced her way, she jerked it higher and smoothed her fingers over her sleek, tightly pulled back hair, as if she'd meant to make the preening gesture all along.

Eugenia made an odd sound, but when Lillian shifted her attention back to her, she went on briskly. "The ivory silk is in the winter closet because Harriet overlooked packing it."

Lillian's suspicions were further aroused when Eugenia went on in an uncharacteristically chatty manner. "Harriet rarely makes mistakes, but we'll forgive her for this one, won't we, particularly if you decide to wear the gown. I want you to look especially fetching tomorrow night. I have some people you must meet."

Her sense that something wasn't right was growing. As Eugenia rambled on about a senator and his son, Lillian's mind was on the ivory silk gown. She was certain the dress she'd never worn was hanging in a wrapper in her Texas apartment. Either Eugenia was mistaken, or something was going on. Her strange behavior just now and Ms. Davies's telling gesture to get

Eugenia's attention, made Lillian eager to get to the winter closet and see the dress for herself.

Ms. Davies suddenly excused herself and left the room. Lillian waited a few moments, then stood to step out of the room herself. Her brief, ''I'll bring us a coffee tray,'' was as close to subterfuge as she'd ever dared.

Once she closed the door behind her, she raced along the hall to the winter closet where their cold weather outerwear was stored. Depending on the deep pile carpet to muffle her footsteps, she arrived just as Ms. Davies closed the door. She slid a key into the keyhole and was about to turn the lock when Lillian touched her arm.

Ms. Davies gave a start and glanced at her, but immediately pulled the key from the lock and moved aside. Lillian stepped past her and pushed the door open. She reached around the corner to switch on the light.

There, hanging on one of the upper sets of clothes rods was the clothing that had been hanging in her closet when she'd left Texas, including the ivory silk gown. The neatly placed boxes at the far end of the huge closet probably contained everything else.

''Well, Ms. Davies,'' Lillian began, retreating behind a facade of stiffness to conceal her hurt and her anger, ''it looks as if Eugenia hasn't quite given up her plans to rule the world.''

''Please, Rye, can I call Lilly? I want to tell her about Buster and the kitten.''

Rye's face felt like stone. Just like his heart. The guilt he felt twisted his gut. He never should have let Joey and Lillian spend time together. He'd been a fool about that, too. Now that Lillian wasn't coming back, Joey would be devastated.

''Lillian's busy with her sick grandma, Joey,'' he said,

trying to avoid as much of the real truth as possible. "It might be hard for her to get to the phone."

The excuse sounded lame to him. Particularly when Lilly had already told him the old witch was doing well. He'd been suspicious right away of the woman's miraculous recovery. He was even more suspicious when two weeks later, poor sick granny still couldn't be left alone with a battalion of nurses and a penthouse full of servants. And now Lillian had sent for her things...

He'd have to prepare Joey, go slow. If there was any way he could let the boy down easily and gradually, he'd find it.

Rye spent extra time with the boy that evening. They played video games and raided the candy drawer. Joey got his shower and Rye supervised his session with the toothbrush. He read Joey another installment of *Treasure Island,* then hovered nearby until he was certain the boy was deeply asleep.

He went straight to the den and tried to call Lillian. The telephone rang more than twenty times before he hung up. He went to the liquor cabinet, selected a glass, then grabbed the thank-you cognac Lillian had left. He was just about to open the bottle and wet his glass when the phone rang.

"Lillian, I insist you be pleasant to me tonight," Eugenia demanded the night of the party as she glared at her granddaughter's reflection in the dresser mirror.

Lillian fussed idly with her hair, using a curling iron to make a few corkscrew curls of the wispy blonde tendrils she'd pulled out of her upswept hairdo.

"Am I not always the soul of pleasantness and repression, Grandmama, dear?" she calmly asked.

Eugenia thumped her cane on the floor in frustration.

"I've only acted in your best interests, young woman. A cattle rancher is no more suitable a match for you than for your sister. And you were working in a bar," she railed on, "a honky-tonk where they sing songs about lowlife cowboys who kiss their horses, sleep with their dogs, and cheat on their big-haired women. I can't tell you how appalled I was to hear that. My God, if anyone here had found out—"

Lillian finished with her hair and gave her grandmother a flat look. "You will refrain from insulting the people who befriended me and criticizing the life I was forced to make, Eugenia. In fact, if you utter one more negative word about any of my life in Texas, I will still attend your party, but I will regale the senator and his son and anyone who will listen with stories about my nights at Uncle Pepper's serving drinks. It might strike my fancy to become creative and spin a tale or two about dancing on the tables or about the night I won the wet T-shirt contest. Fiction, of course, but since I am your granddaughter, I should be able to put on at least as good an act as you did in the hospital."

"Oh!" Eugenia clutched her chest and swayed heavily on her cane. "You mustn't dare, Lillian. Please."

"Then you mustn't dare, dear Grandmama."

Because Lillian was still too angry to trust herself, she turned abruptly from the mirror and stalked from the room.

Lillian was miserable. She had only decided to attend the party because her flight didn't leave until morning. That and because it would serve Eugenia right to worry about what she'd do.

Lillian didn't plan to do anything untoward. She'd

fantasized about it this past twenty-four hours or so, but in the end, she was too well behaved to act on her fantasies.

Once she'd discovered that everything had been moved out of her Texas apartment and shipped to New York, she'd figured out the rest. When she'd confronted her grandmother, Eugenia had arrogantly confessed all, from using the hospital and a minor ulcer problem to make Lillian think she was ill, to the fact that she'd had the bells on all the phones in the penthouse, except her business line, switched off to avoid Rye's calls.

But now that the bells had been turned back on, there still were no calls from Rye. Lillian had almost called him several times, but had thought better of it. Their last phone conversation hadn't gone so well. Besides, Lillian didn't know if he really wanted to speak to her or not.

She was flying to Texas tomorrow for Joey's party on Sunday, but she had no clue now whether Rye would receive her. She'd wait until she got to the little Texas airport, rented a car, then checked into a motel before she called him. Then, if he thought it was better for Joey that she stay out of both their lives, she'd check out of her motel, drive the rental car back to the airport, and fly away somewhere else. The problem was, there was only one place in the world she wanted to be.

So Lillian smiled and made pleasant conversation at the party. She managed to ignore her grandmother in such a way that only Eugenia and Harriet Davies were aware of it. She suffered the introductions to the senator and his son, and though she privately acknowledged that the son was tall and handsome and quite charming, her thoughts on the perfect male had undergone a major transformation.

However suave and debonair the senator's son was,

after Rye, he seemed insincere and somehow weak. His hands were smooth and soft, nothing like the strong, scarred, hard-calloused hands of a certain working rancher. He'd probably never broken a sweat outside a gym, had never overwhelmed a female with his machismo, and never swept a woman off her feet with his shockingly carnal kisses.

He'd probably never considered taking in a lonely, heartbroken little boy and his rambunctious dog, either. He might not be willing to suffer the aggravation and inconvenience of his brother's romantic choice simply because he loved his brother enough to give him time to see the light.

And, because the senator's son had never weathered any real emotional storms or hardships in his life, he'd probably never opened his heart to a woman and let her glimpse the reason for his anger and pain. He may never have learned that for a man to be truly strong, he must make himself vulnerable.

The differences between the two men were stark. More than ever, Lillian ached for Rye. She'd missed him terribly before they'd lost contact, but the last six days with no word from him had been agony. She wished now that she'd bought a new plane ticket last night, after she'd found out about her grandmother's scheme. She could have been in Texas by now, she could already have found out what her chances were of mending things with Rye. As it was, waiting for tomorrow's flight seemed as harsh as a jail term.

Her eyes began to sting suddenly. She made herself smile up at the senator's son—she couldn't recall his name—and politely excused herself. She retreated briefly to the hall on the pretense of primping a bit, but

when she'd regained her composure, she wandered back
to the party. Anything to make the time pass.

Lillian was so beautiful his eyes hurt.

The ivory gown she wore was sleeveless, backless and
flowed over her perfect, slender figure like shimmering
rainwater. With her golden hair piled artfully atop her
head, she had the bearing and appearance of a goddess.

The sight of her humbled him and made him feel like
a bumbling hick. Rye realized then that he'd subcon-
sciously come to think of Lillian in possessive terms,
like some Neanderthal who could barely walk upright.

This first glimpse of her in her finery, standing in this
posh penthouse salon with the elegantly gowned, bejew-
eled and tux-attired elites of New York, made him feel
as if he'd tracked mud on Heaven's white carpet to
snatch away its brightest star.

Could Lillian Renard really be happy with a mere
mortal like him? Could she be satisfied with the much
simpler, rarely glamorous life he could give her?

"Good evening, Mr. Parrish." The pleasantly modu-
lated, cultured voice of the small woman who'd slipped
up beside him gave him a minor start. "What are you
waiting for?"

He turned his head and frowned down at the woman.
"And you are?"

"Harriet Davies, your co-conspirator," she cooed
happily as she turned more fully toward him and held
out her hand to shake his. "And I'm quite pleased to
meet you." Her brown eyes peered up intently at his
face as she continued to hold his hand after the handshake was finished.

"My, but you are an impressive sort of male," she
went on in that low, cultured, delighted voice. "So big

and broad-shouldered and handsome. The boots and Stetson make you look a good foot taller than any man here, but I doubt any of them will give you trouble. I cannot say the same for Eugenia.''

''Where is the old…lady?'' he growled, not truly certain this Ms. Davies was an ally. If he'd had an employee who'd gone behind his back as she had gone behind Eugenia Renard's, he'd have considered staking her out over an anthill.

''Holding court on her throne,'' was the dry response.

Rye glanced in the direction she'd indicated. The silver-haired matron in the lavender dress decorated with matching beadwork, wasn't actually sitting on a throne, but the way she sat perched on the white brocade wing chair, with her hand resting on her tastefully ornate wood and silver cane, was queenly. She held herself in the glamorously arrogant style of a Bette Davis and was far more attractive than he'd expected. But then, he'd expected her to look like the wicked witch from some fairy tale.

He glanced away dismissively and scanned the crowd for Lillian.

As if she were narrating his every move, Ms. Davies said, ''Yes, do look for our dear Lillian. I will move away from you in a moment. That will be your signal to step forward. Your size and manner of dress should successfully hush the crowd and guarantee that every eye is upon you. Once you have Lillian's attention, make some thrillingly romantic speech before you whisk her away. I've already sent her handbag, a wrap and luggage down to the doorman and he will hail you a cab.'' Ms. Davies's voice suddenly sounded choked. ''Good luck to you, sir. Please be good to her.''

And then she was gone, walking toward a spot next to a pillar where she could see everything in the room.

Rye ignored her instruction about making a romantic speech, but he stepped forward and walked straight for Lillian. He got halfway across the floor before the entire room went still. The loud gasp and quick thump-thump-thump he heard from Eugenia's direction brought him to a halt in the center of the floor.

The crowd around him eased back and he felt the curious scrutiny of every eye in the place. He was watching Lillian when she noticed the abrupt silence and turned her head to see the reason.

Lillian couldn't believe her eyes. Rye stood in the center of the crowded room, dressed in a somber black Western suit and bolo tie, his Stetson pitched at a determined angle over his brow. From the crown of his hat to his underslung heels, he was all man, all Texan, and the only man she'd ever love. Was he a mirage?

He extended his hand toward her and spoke her name. "Lillian...are you ready to leave?"

She heard the words, but couldn't move. She couldn't take her eyes from his stern expression. He was speaking to her as if they'd made plans for him to come here and collect her, but her grandmother's harsh, "Lillian!" snagged her attention.

"You will *not* leave here with this...*cowboy*." She turned her silver head and lifted her cane like a royal scepter in the butler's direction. "Ronald! Please call security."

His brisk, "Right away, Madam," preceded his swift disappearance.

Lillian looked back at Rye. As if he were untroubled by Eugenia's order, his blue gaze burned across the room at her. He looked powerful, sure of himself and dangerous. The guests saw it, too. The men kept a wary eye on him, but several of the women smiled and stared at him with feminine appreciation. One or two whispered to a friend.

Rye's hand was still extended to her. Lillian didn't realize she'd started forward until a couple of the guests stepped out of her way.

This was a dream come true, she realized. A glorious, wonderful, romantic dream come to life. As Lillian glided smoothly across the floor, she felt the joy of her love for Rye come bubbling up. Somehow he knew everything, somehow he'd found out about Eugenia's manipulations, somehow he held none of it against her.

Lillian lifted her hand as she neared him. He gently caught her fingers and drew her against him. Lillian stared up at him, thrilled beyond words as he stared down at her. Not a bit of his handsome sternness eased, but the gleam in his eyes was alive with love and desire.

His low, harsh whisper, "I love you, Lilly, come marry me," was audible in the stark silence. It was as if everyone else had suddenly vanished and they were alone in each other's arms in the middle of the floor.

Lillian felt her eyes fill. She was so emotional she couldn't get the words out. She watched, fascinated as his head slowly lowered and his firm lips settled gently on hers. He withdrew slowly and his arm tightened around her.

"Come marry me, Lilly. Be my wife."

Lillian's soft, "Yes, yes..." was all it took for Rye to ease her away from him. Still holding her hand, he raised it to his lips in silent tribute, his eyes still burning down at her as he kissed her knuckle.

And then he swept her into his arms, turned and strode confidently from the salon to the foyer in front of the elevator. The crowd rushed out after them, but stopped a respectful distance when Rye stopped to wait for the elevator door to open.

Lillian leaned close and whispered in his ear. Obediently, he turned so she could face the crowd.

"Please, will all of you excuse Mr. Parrish and me?" she asked with a voice that had gone breathless with excitement. "In future, I may be reached at the Parrish Ranch in Texas. I shall be pleased to answer any correspondence addressed to Mrs. Rye Parrish." The soft tone that signaled the elevator's arrival made her pause. "Thank you all for being such gracious guests. Goodbye all!"

Lillian looked up into Rye's face. His eyes glittered down at her, his harsh expression softened by amusement and pride. He turned from the crowd and stepped onto the elevator with his prize.

The elevator door closed to the sound of applause.

EPILOGUE

ONE month later, the main house at Parrish Ranch was crowded with wedding guests. All of Lillian's new friends were there, plus a surprising number of friends from New York. Rachel hadn't responded to her wedding invitation and neither had Eugenia, but Harriet Davies had arrived two days earlier. Her help with last-minute details had been invaluable.

To plan the large ten a.m. wedding in one short month had been nothing short of insanity, but hiring a Dallas wedding planner had helped. Chad would be Rye's best man, and Lexie, the single friend who'd worked with Lillian at Uncle Pepper's, would be her bridesmaid. Joey would be their ring bearer and Dovey had not only baked and professionally decorated the towering wedding cake, he'd organized the reception and the huge barbecue that would follow at one o'clock. Buster had been safely locked away in a shed.

It was now almost nine-thirty a.m. The florists had just finished constructing the rose arbor on the patio. Hundreds of pink and white roses were clustered down the support poles and formed the ceiling and roof of the arbor, which would provide the only shade for Rye and Lillian as they took their vows in the center of the patio near the pool. The guests were being seated under the huge roof overhangs and inside the rooms whose double doors opened onto the patio. The organist was playing softly, and everything was ready.

Joey had already rushed back and forth between Rye's

room and Lillian's so often that Ms. Davies warned him he'd wear out the carpets. But the moment Rye and Chad helped him on with the miniature version of the tuxedos they would wear, he managed to actually sit still a few moments longer between trips.

Twenty minutes before the ceremony, Ms. Davies had just helped Lillian put on her headpiece when they heard a fresh commotion in the hall.

"Which room is my granddaughter in?"

The imperious voice carried to Lillian's door. Startled, she and Ms. Davies glanced at one another.

Lillian's low, "You don't think she'll try to disrupt the ceremony, do you?" betrayed her fear.

Ms. Davies frowned, but hurried to the hall and closed the door quietly behind her. Lillian was suddenly more nervous than ever. By the time Harriet tapped on the door and opened it, her nerves were screaming.

That was when Joey knocked on the connecting door, opened it wide enough to squeeze through, then shoved it shut. At the same moment, Eugenia marched into the room from the hall and came to a halt.

The instant Eugenia saw the boy in the tiny tuxedo, her scowl deepened. She leaned forward a bit on her cane to peer at him before she straightened and glared at Lillian.

"Whose child is this and what on earth is he doing in this room?" she demanded.

Knowing Joey wouldn't understand her grandmother's rudeness, she walked over and placed a gentle hand on his shoulder. She smiled down at him to let him know everything was all right before she looked up and answered her grandmother.

"Grandmama, this is Joey Parrish. Rye is his guardian and we are in the process of adopting him. He'll be our ring bearer today.'' She looked down at Joey. ''Joey, this is my grandmother, Eugenia.''

At her gentle nudge, Joey started forward and walked closer to Eugenia. His, ''Quite pleased to meet you, ma'am,'' was stiff and clearly memorized and thoroughly charming.

Eugenia's penciled brows winged high as she looked down at him. ''Yes...well—see that you are, young man. Particularly if I must bear the duty of being your great-grandmama. I would like a chair. Please fetch one.''

Joey dashed across the room, grabbed the spare dining room chair they'd brought in earlier, then pulled it across the carpet to Eugenia.

''No, not here,'' Eugenia grumbled. ''Over there.'' She pointed to a space by the French doors.

Joey obediently placed the chair exactly where Eugenia had pointed. ''Now,'' she said, ''if you will sit on that chair and not muss yourself or chatter, you shall not make me nervous.''

She turned fully toward Lillian, who stood with stiff poise in her wedding finery. The head-to-toe scrutiny Lillian endured only added to her nervousness. Eugenia made a slight motion with her hand to prompt Lillian to make a slow turn. Lexie stepped forward to catch the end of Lillian's long veil to help her manage it.

''You, bridesmaid,'' Eugenia called when the turn was complete. ''What is your name, please?''

Lexie glanced up, a bit wary of Eugenia.

''I'm sorry, Grandmama,'' Lillian said quickly. ''This is my friend Lexie Warner. Lexie, this is my grandmother, Eugenia Renard.''

''Nice to meet you, ma'am,'' Lexie murmured.

"You are a pretty young woman, Ms. Warner. Perhaps you will catch the bridal bouquet."

Lexie seemed to relax at that and smiled. "Yes, ma'am, maybe so."

The tension in the room was fierce. Eugenia stepped a bit closer to Lillian. She paused to give Lexie a meaningful stare. Lexie slipped away and walked to the French doors to peek out the drapes. Once she and Lillian had as much privacy as possible, Eugenia spoke.

"It looks as if you are truly going to marry this…gentleman," she said. "I've never cared for divorce, so I hope you've made certain this is a permanent arrangement."

"I have, Grandmama," she said softly. "I wish you would get to know him."

"Yes, perhaps. His home is certainly impressive. Perhaps he's not quite the country bumpkin I first thought." She lifted her chin. "I would like the name of your photographer. I should like to order a full set of wedding photos and enlargements. It's not every day I have a granddaughter who gets married, you know."

Lillian stared into her grandmother's eyes and felt her emotions rise. Perhaps this was as close as Eugenia could come to giving her blessing.

"Does this mean you approve?"

"You do not need my approval to marry this man, Lillian. However, I would not travel to this godforsaken frontier and abide the heat and the dust if it were not important to me to be here." Eugenia's voice suddenly had a suspicious hoarseness. "I came to see my beautiful granddaughter properly married to the man of her choice."

Eugenia's gaze glimmered and something softened in

her normally severe expression. "And...I do approve, my dear. I wish you all the best."

Lillian spontaneously reached for her grandmother's hand, surprised when Eugenia reached for hers. "Thank you, Grandmama. You don't know how much it means to me," she whispered.

"God knows why you'd give a fig for anything I think, Lillian," she whispered back, her voice betraying an emotional tremor. "I've been a dreadful grandmama."

A fat tear shot down Lillian's cheek and Eugenia drew back appalled. "Don't cry, silly bride!" she said urgently. "Harriet, bring a tissue!"

Five minutes after solving the minor crisis, Chad came for Joey. Dovey came to escort Eugenia to a place of honor in the shade where she could view of the faces of her granddaughter and her groom as they took their vows.

At the signal, an usher opened the French doors of Lillian's bedroom. Lexie stepped out onto the patio and waited while Joey walked slowly along the carpeted path to the arbor. She walked slowly after him, then took her position beneath the arbor.

As the organist began the first note of "Here Comes the Bride," Lillian stepped forward, her heart bursting with joy.

Rye waited beneath the fragrant rose arbor for his bride. Lillian was beautiful. As she glided regally toward him in a white cloud of satin and lace, seed pearls and silk veils, she seemed ethereal. The bright sunlight on her gown was blinding, adding to the notion that he'd tracked all the way to heaven and brought back its brightest star.

Somehow, every hurt he'd ever suffered, every disappointment he'd ever endured, was being soothed to-day. Healed. This woman who would be his wife was as gentle and sweet a soul as he'd ever met. Just being with her gave him ease, cheered him. If he could give her half as much happiness as she'd given him, she'd never have another sad moment in her life.

Before she reached the rose arbor, he stepped forward and caught her fingers. She gripped his hand and he could feel her tremble. Together, they stepped beneath the roses, turned to the minister, then solemnly pledged their love and lives...

Later, after the reception and barbecue, after Harriet Davies caught the bridal bouquet, and the bride and groom departed for their honeymoon beneath a hail of birdseed, Buster dug his way out of the shed and had the unexpected pleasure of making Eugenia Renard's ac-quaintance.

Head Down Under for twelve tales of heated romance in beautiful and untamed Australia!

Here's a sneak preview of the first novel in
THE AUSTRALIANS

Outback Heat **by Emma Darcy**
available July 1998

'HAVE I DONE something wrong?' Angie persisted, wishing Taylor would emit a sense of camaraderie instead of holding an impenetrable reserve.

'Not at all,' he assured her. 'I would say a lot of things right. You seem to be fitting into our little Outback community very well. I've heard only good things about you.'

'They're nice people,' she said sincerely. Only the Maguire family kept her shut out of their hearts.

'Yes,' he agreed. 'Though I appreciate it's taken considerable effort from you. It is a world away from what you're used to.'

The control Angie had been exerting over her feelings snapped. He wasn't as blatant as his aunt in his prejudice against her but she'd felt it coming through every word he'd spoken and she didn't deserve any of it.

'Don't judge me by your wife!'

His jaw jerked. A flicker of some dark emotion destroyed the steady power of his probing gaze.

'No two people are the same. If you don't know that, you're a man of very limited vision. So I come from the city as your wife did! That doesn't stop me from being an individual in my own right.'

She straightened up, proudly defiant, furiously angry with the situation. 'I'm *me*. Angie Cordell. And it's time you took the blinkers off your eyes, Taylor Maguire.'

Then she whirled away from him, too agitated by the explosive expulsion of her emotion to keep facing him.

The storm outside hadn't yet eased. There was nowhere to go. She stopped at the window, staring blindly at the torrential rain. The thundering on the roof was almost deafening but it wasn't as loud as the silence behind her.

'You want me to go, don't you? You've given me a month's respite and now you want me to leave and channel my energies somewhere else.'

'I didn't say that, Angie.'

'You were working your way around it.' Bitterness at his tactics spewed the suspicion. 'Do you have your first choice of governess waiting in the wings?'

'No. I said I'd give you a chance.'

'Have you?' She swung around to face him. 'Have you really, Taylor?'

He hadn't moved. He didn't move now except to make a gesture of appeasement. 'Angie, I was merely trying to ascertain how you felt.'

'Then let me tell you your cynicism was shining through every word.'

He frowned, shook his head. 'I didn't mean to hurt you.' The blue eyes fastened on hers with devastating sincerity. 'I truly did not come in here to take you down or suggest you leave.'

Her heart jiggled painfully. He might be speaking the truth but the judgements were still there, the judgements that ruled his attitude towards her, that kept her shut out of his life, denied any real sharing with him, denied his confidence and trust. She didn't know why it meant so much to her but it did. It did. And the need to fight for justice from him was as much a raging torrent inside her as the rain outside.

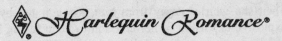

Harlequin Romance®

Get ready to meet the world's most eligible bachelors: they're sexy, successful and, best of all, they're all yours!

BACHELOR TERRITORY

Look out for these next two books:

May 1998: ONE BRIDE REQUIRED! (#3505) by Emma Richmond

Tycoon Nash Vallender has decided it's time for him to settle down. He has the house, the fortune, all he needs is the right woman. Enter Phoenix Langrish. Aside from being a gorgeous leggy brunette, Phoenix is also the only woman he's ever come close to loving. There's just one problem—she has no intention of becoming Nash's bride!

July 1998: THE BACHELOR AND THE BABIES (#3513) by Heather MacAllister

When Harrison Rothwell is left holding his brother's baby—well, two babies to be exact—he decides to demonstrate that his rules of business management can be applied to any situation. Trouble is his tiny nephews won't take orders from any boss! Which is where Carrie Brent comes in. She may be totally disorganized but when it comes to rug-rats, she's a natural! Can she convince Harrison that rules are made to be broken?

There are two sides to every relationship— and now it's his turn!

Take 4 bestselling love stories FREE

Plus get a FREE surprise gift!

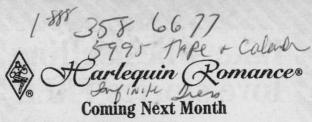

1 888 358 6677
5995 Tape + Calendar
Soft inite Dress

Coming Next Month

#3511 BIRTHDAY BRIDE Jessica Hart
Sexy, glamorous... Claudia tried to think of three good things about
turning thirty. Having to pretend to be David Stirling's bride wasn't
one of them. But for the next few weeks she was stuck with him and
the pretense. And perhaps, at her age, sexy, glamorous and *wed* was an
improvement?

We're delighted to bring you a special new series in Harlequin Romance
and Presents all about...

The Big Event! *One special occasion—that changes your life forever.*

#3512 A KISS FOR JULIE Betty Neels
Julie enjoyed her work as a medical secretary, so it was a nasty surprise
when her elderly boss announced he was retiring. She was partly
reassured when told that Professor Simon van der Driesma was willing to
keep her on—but Simon turned out to be a very different proposition....

#3513 THE BACHELOR AND THE BABIES Heather MacAllister
When Harrison Rothwell is left holding his brother's baby—well, two
babies to be exact—he decides to demonstrate that his rules of business
management can be applied to any situation. Trouble is, his tiny
nephews won't take orders from any boss! Which is where Carrie Brent
comes in. She may be totally disorganized but when it comes to rug
rats—she's a natural! Can she convince Harrison that rules are made to
be broken?

Get ready to meet the world's most eligible bachelors: they're sexy,
successful and, best of all, they're all yours!

Bachelor Territory: *There are two sides to every story...and now it's
his turn!*

#3514 LAST CHANCE MARRIAGE Rosemary Gibson
After one disastrous marriage, Clemency Adams had vowed to
give up men and concentrate on her career. Her next-door neighbor,
Joshua Harrington, was equally determined not to marry again.
Unfortunately, these new neighbors were finding it difficult to fight
their growing attraction for one another....